Shavori,

You are ray
light in
this world!

♡ TJ

From Darkness to Light

LINDSEY LEWIS

authorHOUSE®

AuthorHouse™
1663 Liberty Drive
Bloomington, IN 47403
www.authorhouse.com
Phone: 1 (800) 839-8640

Published by AuthorHouse   04/20/2016

ISBN: 978-1-5049-7136-2 (sc)
ISBN: 978-1-5049-7135-5 (e)

Library of Congress Control Number: 2016900461

Print information available on the last page.

For: you. Yes, you.

I have attempted at all times to be factual but have changed names and identifying details to protect individuals' privacy. Except for Matthew—he's exactly as he is. Conversations and the timeline of events are written from memory, and some dialogue is crafted from my memory of the impact of what was said. And, when using the term 'God', it's a more cosmic than personified version.

Prologue

The bed is cold. There aren't enough blankets. Even though the weight of the ones I'm under presses me into the mattress, freezes me in time and space. Nothing exists beyond this moment—no past, no future—nothing but this pounding head, crawling skin, and vice around my chest. I inhale. Count "one, two, three, four, five…" I reach thirty before I gasp for breath. The hammering in my head returns.

Again.

Inhale. Count "one, two, three, four, five…" This time, I reach forty before the tension is too much. Gasp for air. Punch the blankets.

One more time.

Inhale. Count "one, two, three, four, five…" I reach fifty.

But there's no respite. No slipping into darkness. No peace. The hammer is relentless. I am wide awake. Watching my mind ricochet, roller-coaster, spin out in unceasing circles. Feeling my muscles cling, hold tight. They're never letting go.

I am dying for this to end. More than that. To free myself. To slip from the shackles of the manic vigilance of a nervous system gone haywire—out into nothingness.

Instead, I am here. Still here.

Sunshine breaks through the clouds, yellow streamers between tufts of gray, touching the treetops, slipping between the branches, illuminating the leaves. Hundreds of shades of green. One tree stands taller than the rest, arching solid branches ever outward, sometimes resting one tip on another tree's limb. An aged mother. One branch in particular has stretched longer than the others, gives the tree the look of a directional beacon, always pointing. At the tip of this branch is a bud, a softest green. It wiggles a little. There is no breeze.

The bud shifts, expands as though with breath, and then begins to descend. Down toward the trunk. Inch by inch. It's not a bud, but a caterpillar. So green she seems a newly unfurled leaf. So soft she seems brand new. She pauses, rises up from her middle, and casts her eyes around her. She sees shades of darkness and light—no clear images. Up ahead, the darkness beckons. She moves toward it. Inch by inch.

Chapter 1

Even the air feels bright. There is a crispness in the sunshine that speaks of falling leaves, gloves and boots, scarves wrapped around necks, and collars turned up. Unlike summer, with its haze of warmth and endless days, early fall throws everything into stark contrast: shadows seem darker, the sky higher, and everywhere there is the emerging palette of oranges, yellows, and reds.

The deepest red of them all is at my feet—the carpet that lies on the sidewalk. I flash my smile to the man behind the camera. Pop! The flash bursts. At the door I give my name to the girl in six-inch heels and a black shift dress.

It's not that there are fans who want to see my picture in print. I'm a magazine editor. I'm not famous. It's not for the owners of the eatery we are converging at—the newest development from Vancouver's hottest restaurant group—either. They don't really care to look at shot after shot of the people who attended their party. The pictures, one after the other—pop! flash! "Great!"— are being taken for those of us on the receiving end. So we can feel we are famous, that people want to look at pictures of us, that on this night we are living the dream.

That's what gets us out weeknight after weeknight, has us saying yes to hours of standing around in shoes that pinch and hair that can't be touched. If we didn't go? If we missed the event of the week, the month, the year? Everyone would think we weren't worthy.

So we fill the rooms. Lounging in banquets, leaning against cocktail tables, one hip on the edge of a barstool, we are all there—the city's influencers. In a burgundy dress, hair piled high, a television host leans against a pillar, looking but pretending not to. The magazine editor-in-chiefs aren't there but their editors are, polished and buffed, their skirts, pants and tops sourced from up-and-coming online sites or gifted from a line's publicist. Columnists for the major newspapers dress in more muted tones and carry a slightly tread-worn air. The social column writer is taking notes, calling across the room, and every now and then touching the arm of someone who walks by; they will stop and lean in, nod at his comments and laugh at his jokes, some of them lingering, fawning.

The media. They shine in photograph after photograph, are used to seeing their name in print, casually mentioned once again at the latest hottest restaurant, shop, play opening, charity event, fashion show, or nightclub. Talking to them is a game of quick jabs, *bons mots*, and smiles that don't spread to the eyes. Dropping short sentences that they can easily digest as their eyes roam the room to see who else is there.

Others are genuinely happy, honestly at ease, standing comfortably at the bar or in a quiet corner of the room, sharing conversation. They are the people who love their craft more than the perks that come along with it, focusing more on their skill than the lifestyle it enables, in an industry that the new president of the biggest media company in the country recently deemed "the most fun you can have legally."

Servers in white shirts and short black skirts or tailored slacks circle the room with trays stacked with duck confit gnocchi, rosemary beef ravioli, and ciabatta bread with truffle honey. It is a consciously inventive take on traditional Italian, and La Fermosa is the newest restaurant from the hottest nightlife and restaurant developer in the city. The invitation had arrived from the publicist, one of many that came in every week, filled with exaggeration.

> Everyone will be there. Jet-setters. Trend-setters.
> It's the new place to see and be seen.
> Hope to see you there!
> Best,
> Carrie

And I want to be here. Of course I do. I want to be near these beautiful people. Want to have my picture taken, see my name in print, catch a glimpse of myself in the "Around Town" section. I'd straightened my bob, slicked on lip gloss, and layered on foundation. Crammed my feet into heels that boosted me from five foot nine to six foot one.

Today, with the taxi waiting outside, I had kissed Joseph goodbye as a wave of nausea washed over me, imagining a time when an evening like this wouldn't make me feel like I was turning inside out. I'd been faking confidence for years. It started when I was fourteen and I've been perfecting it ever since. It's something you learn quickly, when your panic attacks are as big as your dreams.

Now, surrounded by beautiful people, I force a smile, press my shoulders back and my head high, arrange my limbs on a stool, holding them in a way I hope looks casual.

Inhale. Count "one, two, three, four, five…"

Chapter 2

I have a corner office. It has a view. Not of city lights or the jutting rooftops of skyscrapers. The courtyard I look out over is serene and simple, a spot to sit and read a book, or eat your lunch in the sun. I bus to work, walking the last four blocks down toward the office on the edge of the water. My route takes me past million-dollar condos, peekaboo views of the inlet, and under Chinese maple trees. The stairs down to my office begin in a green haven, with ferns and stones laid carefully underfoot. Each day this place invites me to pause, to look out over the inlet, downtown, and the glass-fronted buildings edging the curve of the seawall.

On sunny days, everything shines.

We publish one of the most profitable magazines in the roster of one of the country's biggest magazine publishing houses. The visitor magazine details where to go, what to do, and what to buy—and this means that we editors get to do and see everything there is to do and see, for free. Opening night parties are a regular part of our week. We eat complimentary lunches or dinners at the city's top restaurants. We are invited to spend the night at the hotels everyone is talking about, and get massaged, buffed, and moisturized at free spa treatments a few times a month. Make-up and home accessories regularly arrive via courier.

So why don't I feel OK? Why do I spend each moment in a war with myself?

The morning after the party at La Fermosa, I arrive late for the first time. Everyone else is already there, even Edna, the editor-in-chief. Everyone else is already working, keyboards tick-tapping, the silence of focus a container I step into when I come through the door. My shoes are loud on the floor, the scrape of my chair a siren call, the uprising tune of my computer turning on too brash and bright in the midst of all this concentration. There is a voice in my head and it is terrified: *You were late. Of course they noticed.*

The voice gets louder. The silence around me grows thick. The pounding of my heart rises to my head. In an instant, red begins to color everything I see. "Morning, Linds." The pounding joins forces with the red—a relentless, endless swarm. I press my palms into the surface of my desk, close my eyes, breathe in, breathe out.

"Linds?" Behind me. It's Brian, the art director. I can make out the timbre in his voice. The voice in my head grows quiet. The swarm fades away. He is talking about the title I've written for a story; it's too long for the space on the page. He wonders if I can create something different. Is that OK with me?

Here is something to latch onto: yes, that's OK with me. I can do that. I can do this. Text fits into copy boxes, words relay themselves through my fingers and my mind has something to land on again. It begins to return from its unceasing circles. I can hear birds in the trees outside.

That afternoon I'm leaning on the fence lining the boardwalk that juts out into the harbour where the sailboats anchor. Sails spun around masts, covers snapped on tight, dock lines wrapped in an infinity symbol around cleats, the boats are protected against any rain or wind and simply bob in place. The face of an old man rises from the waters beside them and it's a seal, dark fur slick with wet and whiskers framing a button nose. Gulls circle and cry out.

I'm here, but there's a layer between me and what's right in front of me, a thick fog that stifles my breath and clouds my vision. I carry it with me always. Anxiety is like an oversize life jacket that instead of boosting me up makes me feel like I'm drowning. Sometimes, being in a peaceful place makes it worse; there's less to distract me from the rising tide of knowing that, despite having gotten it all right, everything is wrong.

I haven't slept. Of course I haven't. I lie awake going over everything I have left to do to meet all my deadlines. For the entire year. I'm convinced I'll miss something, that I already have, that I'll be called into Edna's office and the publisher will be there and together they will list off every mistake I've made.

It doesn't matter that Edna is truly and sincerely kind at all times, has the crinkly eyes of someone always in on the joke. Edna has been an actress for years, as well as a writer. She will sail into the office and tiny firecrackers speed into the corners of the room and light it up. She loves her craft—to have your work edited by her is to experience the gentle nudge of your skill up to its next level—and the perks that come with it.

At the theatre on opening night she is brighter than the stars of the show—kissing cheeks with old friends and actors she'd been on stage with, head back, throat bared to a laugh that turns the heads of those around her. She is still talking, leaning in to rush through a breathless conversation almost until the curtain goes up. The next morning she sits tall and focused at her desk, glasses pressed up on the bridge of her nose, typing out an e-mail or edits to be sent to a freelancer.

Edna and I often talk about our inability to sleep, how we lie awake at night aching for rest and relief from our racing minds. Hot milk with honey, yoga postures with our feet above our heads, no chocolate after three in the afternoon—we've both tried it all. I am weaning myself off sleeping pills, wrenching myself from my love affair with the tiny white disc I pop under my tongue to slide from the shackles of adrenaline that feel otherwise impossible to escape. I started using them in my last semester of university, having begged my doctor for a prescription to stop the torture of lying awake night after night—inhaling, counting, and still no respite—with one day running straight into the next, and the next, and the next; an endless, horror-film loop.

Edna and I swap stories of nights spent tangled in sheets or stalking our apartments in the dark, wide-eyed and strung-out, our sleeping partners blissfully unaware

From Darkness to Light

that we are silently cursing them for their innocent ability to do something that does not in the least come naturally to us.

"It is so nice, isn't it?" A small man appears beside me, inhaling the view. With his Greek accent, tanned, bald head, and wide grin, he makes me think of an oversize child. Dressed in white, he stands with his hands at his waist—browned skin thick and spotted, white hairs speckled over the surface—gazing out beyond the boats in front of us. I nod, smiling back, and push away from the railing. He follows.

"It reminds me of my island. On my island there are so many boats. There, you can see the ocean go on forever." He sighs. "I walk this pathway every day," proudly puffing his chest, swinging his arms and striding to keep up. "I have seen you here before, but you didn't used to be here." Looking up through curious eyes.

There is something in his look. It's a kindness that conveys a depth, a light that is compassionate. It pulls that part of me forward, so that I begin to feel softer, gentler, calm.

"I started working at a magazine near here. Do you know it?"

"Tell me about it," he says.

So I do, arcing along the story of how I became a magazine editor, how I was lucky to get a position, and so soon. "I'm really lucky." I say it twice. The small Greek man looks at me sideways, a question on his face. But he doesn't voice it. Instead, he asks my name, takes my hand between both of his, kisses the top of it and lets it go.

"Lindsey, I am Iairos. It has been so nice to meet you. I hope we meet again."

On the bus ride home I imagine Greece—all blues and whites with shades of green and pink. I imagine lying on a beach, really being there. Without my mind taking me spinning. Just there. Sand beneath me. Sky above. Breathing it in.

Our street is like an advertisement for fall. There are shades of orange and red and yellow everywhere—on the trees, at my feet, piled on the neighbors' lawns. The moon is starting to take over the sky.

Dinner is mostly red, too: spaghetti with whole wheat noodles and a side salad. I fill three-quarters of my plate with greens. Today, I got my favorite kind of invitation—an invitation to go on a trip. For free. I'm telling Joseph all about it: the most luxurious train trip in the world. A trip some people save for for years. I remember when I thought I hadn't gotten the internship that got me here.

The living room carpet had been cool beneath my back. I stared at a crack in the ceiling, brown dashes lining it on either side; it looked like a crevice in the earth of another land, and the dashes tiny people being pulled down into the darkness. I closed my eyes. The sound of a key turning in the lock woke me up and I curled over onto my side away from the front door. Joseph curled himself behind me and I could hear him breathing.

"I didn't get it."

"How do you know?"

"I blew the last question. The best question."

Visions of spending the rest of my life temping rose up to cast shadows on the wall. I saw myself at sixty, gray-haired, with talons for nails, dressed in a polyester navy-blue pantsuit. "James Jones International, how can I help you?"

"Maybe you'll still get it." Joseph rested his head on my cheek. I shook my head. He flipped around until he could look me in the eye. "Maybe you will."

Those eyes. I hadn't noticed them until our last year of high school. And then, suddenly, he was there, standing in front of my desk in English class asking if I wanted to partner on a poetry project.

Head bent over my desk, I had felt him before I saw him, a sense of something smooth and soothing anchoring me in place. I looked up. Into gray eyes under feather-light lashes. The other weekend I'd been out with my friend Maria and her boyfriend, and his friend—a Spanish guy with rings and tattoos—ran his hand up the length of my arm, tipping my chin toward him: "Why don't you talk?" he'd asked.

My stomach twisted into knots. "I don't know what to say."

Joseph and I met at my house for our first attempt at getting started on the poetry project and spent the entire afternoon talking, asking each other question after question across my parent's dining room table. "Where did you grow up?" "Do you have any brothers or sisters?" "What do you want to do when you graduate?" He had one older brother and a dog named Bravo, and when he graduated he wanted to become an astronaut. Before

Joseph's dad came to pick him up we looked at what we'd completed: a paragraph or so of notes, some wiggly shaded lines, a few smiley faces.

Tonight, I say, "I'm excited."

Joseph's smile is tight, but he hugs me and says, "That's great."

Chapter 3

Iairos is endlessly curious about my trip. His questions come from a place inside him where there is space for every story from every person he meets, where each adventure I tell him about becomes one he gets to go on, too. It seems that having met once we are destined to meet again. And again. He appears beside me. We walk side by side, sometimes talking, sometimes just listening. Watching the water reflect the sky and the boats come and go. The people on bicycles streaming past and the dogs on leashes straining against them.

Iairos is always dressed in white.

He sometimes talks about Greece. "Back home" is a place where everything is simple. Where the warmth of the earth reflects the heat of the sun. Where there is no hurry. No rush. And the saltwater holds you up. He wants to hear about the Rocky Mountains.

"They stand like giants. There's something about them—the way they seem both fierce and protective at the same time. The train will go along right beside them. We'll see them rise up from the prairies." I tell Iairos how each of the first-class cars has a glass top so that no part of the landscape is blocked from view. How even in the second-class cars you're served and entertained and have everything taken care of for you. That I heard it's the most expensive train trip in North America. That they're putting me up in two hotels, for free. It's all free. Just because I'm an editor.

"Lindsey, so long as you are happy." Iairos has eyes that catch flecks of light when he looks up.

I take a taxi to the airport, which I love more than being dropped off by someone I know because it makes me feel even more like I'm in New York City. And another to the hotel I'm staying at in the city I fly into the night before I board the train. People-watching from the window of a cab is like filming a movie—each person framed through the arced window appears more like an archetype than an actual person. I arrived in the dark, so the figures crossing the streets and huddling into building entryways are shapes that can be filled in by my imagination—stories of sisters, lovers, ex-husbands and wives play out across the rear passenger window as the cab winds down the emptying streets.

In the morning, I imagine a star like Ingrid Bergman boarding the train; Hollywood scenes of high drama in small spaces play across my mind. Inside, red-velvet seats with high backs sit four to a row with an aisle down the middle. I have two to myself and lay my notebooks, laptop, and purse on the seat beside me. The fixtures are brass and somebody has spent a lot of time buffing them. The windows glint. There is a scent of lemon: the cleaning product used to shampoo the seats. Around me in the other seats are men and women from Europe, Australia, and New Zealand—but mostly the United States.

A silver-haired man with wire-rimmed glasses and a New Zealand accent is the first to ask me: "Who are you?" I don't blame him. I think I'm the only single woman on an entire train full of older couples. That I've been invited to ride the train by the company that runs it makes him laugh. "Can't complain about that job, hey?" I don't complain. I watch the couples who are traveling together. The way they lean their heads toward each other, the way one will order for the other if he or she has gone to the bathroom, not hesitating for a breath about choosing, knowing that they know what the other will want. I watch the way they communicate through looks when they're not sitting close enough to talk.

It's odd that I'm here on my own. As I walk by, people pretend to be reading or looking out the window but give me sidelong glances. Others look up at me, nudging their travel partner.

Not everyone onboard is silver-haired. Angus, from Scotland, is in his early forties, and, he tells me, spent years saving up for his one big trip across Canada. He's married but here on his own, having left his wife and kids for two weeks. He tells me this gleefully, a kid skipping out of school. He's always loved animals, even as a kid, and this is why he's on this particular trip, on this particular train. He spends all of the time between meals scanning the bushes from the portico, camera trigger-ready.

Crash. The doors bang open and Angus's red hair and mustache lead the way for his face as it peers into our car. He yells out "Bear!" before slamming back out to snap picture after picture. The bears, as cuddly looking as they are ferocious, trundle up the hillside and into the cover of the trees as fast as they can. Comfortable in our seats, the rest of us watch them go.

"Would you like a drink, miss?" One of two white-shirted staff members assigned to our car is rolling out refreshments. We tuck our snacks into compartments and listen as the tour guide points out trees, rockslides, and skeletons of buildings that used to make up small towns. I remember this. For years each summer my family and I would drive this route the opposite direction, to visit my grandparents, and even though it's appearing in reverse this landscape has the same effect as it did when I was a kid: it soothes me. The constant rhythm of the train across the tracks does too, and soon my head is lolling and my mouth dropping open even though each time I jolt awake I try to make sure it's closed.

Crash! The doors bang open again and Angus hollers "Deer!" before turning on his heel to get back into position. The rest of us catch the flick of a white tail raised in alarm as the deer lopes into the trees, vanishing into the forest. Angus is delighting people. When he disappears back into his picture-taking station, there is a low hum of comments paired with big smiles and head-shaking. I get the sense that Angus is creating for himself the experience that each of the people on this train signed up for. And because of him, they're closer to getting it. When he finally comes in for a break, multiple people ask if he got the shots he wanted, is he happy with what he's seen so far, can they see the pictures.

Angus leans over, pointing to one image and then the next, ears lifting at the tips to pull his face into a wide smile. Row after row of twosomes want to see what he captured, ask him the temperature outside, listen to his Scots accent as he shares everything he knows about the animals he's seen. It takes ages for him to get back to his seat.

Not long after he does, the announcement is made: We've arrived at our overnight stop, a small town not far from the Pacific coast. My elbow is in the palm of the hand belonging to the man in a navy blue uniform who brought the drinks. He is guiding me off the train and showing me where to wait for my bags. A woman in blue with a ponytail high on her head stands waiting, smiling, and when my bags are delivered lifts them into the taxi. I get in. She slaps the door with her palm.

"Which way are we headed?" I ask the driver.

"To the top of the hill."

The town and river grow smaller beneath us and the car climbs to a hotel overlooking the valley: the brick buildings of Main St., the heritage homes cozy in the center, the newer ones rimming the edge and spreading beyond the banks of the river, climbing up the hills until they peter out, replaced by sagebrush and grassland. At the entrance, a bellhop waits and greets me by name, takes my suitcase and walks me to my room—all muted tones and large windows with an oversize duvet and piles of pillows on the bed. On the desk sits a welcome basket with chocolates, nuts, and candied fruit, as well as a handwritten note signed by the manager of the hotel: "Lindsey, I hope that you enjoy your stay."

I strip off my clothes, the smell of the cleaner and sandwiches, and dive onto the bed. There is a giant bath in the bathroom and a seafood salad on the room service menu. When it arrives I eat it in my underwear, down duvet pillowed around my lap. Afterward, steam from the hot water I fill the bath with thickens the air. One toe tries it out first and then I sink in up to my neck and, inhaling deep, slide until I'm immersed; the water resonates with the beating of my heart.

That night, I sleep long and deep, waking just in time to pack my bag and dress before my morning pick-up. The taxi slides back down the hill, through the condos, houses, and heritage homes, past the brick buildings of Main St., to the train station.

It's a tall, dark-haired staffer named Lou who takes my luggage, hands it off, and then takes my elbow. I'm in the front row, on the very first of the glass-ceilinged two-story cars that snake behind us, single-story cars behind them. There is a dining room below. One of our onboard servers hands me a champagne glass. My mimosa.

Behind me that day sits a golden-haired grandmother and her fluffy-haired golden grandson. I know they're from the southern United States not just because of the drawl. It's the way she sits like I imagine a Southern matriarch in a movie would, with her perfectly turned cuffs and string of pearls with matching earrings. She ducks her chin to murmur in her grandson's ear about what they see out the window. When she points to something, though, it's him, not her, who labels it.

The quiet is a weight that keeps us all in our seats—there's no Scottish man bursting in, no jokes called out from one seat to the next or eruptions of laughter, just a low murmur of conversation and the clinking of champagne glasses. For the first part of the morning, I'm ensconced by the arms and high back of my seat.

I journal, write whatever comes to mind, draft notes on what I've seen so far, and outline my ideas for stories for the magazine. I also do something that feels sneaky, almost illicit. I record everything I notice about the most interesting people around me. The Southern matriarch. Her grandson. The German and American couples traveling together. They laugh as though they've known each other for years, and through times that made them grow close. I imagine them stuck in an airport on another trip, their plane having been delayed, giddy with tiredness, oscillating between being cranky and gently mocking each other when they are.

The deep quiet lasts until brunch is served on the first floor of the car, at round tables with pressed tablecloths and flower centerpieces. I join the German and American foursome.

"We are all wondering," begins the American man with the glasses that can only be called spectacles because of the way they sit on the end of his nose. "You are here on your own . . ." And then, when I don't answer, "Where's your boyfriend?"

"He doesn't come."

One night in bed, early in our relationship, Joseph and I had mapped out a life for ourselves with him as a photographer, by my side on trips just like this. But both of us knew it was just fantasy; his dreams don't really intersect with mine. This thought pulls at the center of my mind and lands with a kick in my heart, and I think back to the last time Joseph and I fought, a couple months ago. All that week I had been anxious, tense with worry about upcoming deadlines, consumed with thoughts of each task on my to-do list, convinced I would never get it all done. And on this particular night I was lying awake, wondering where he was.

I could have guessed, could have assumed, that he'd gone for drinks with his friends after his tae kwon do class, could have been happy he was doing something that made him so happy, and let it go. But I was furious. Furious that he hadn't called to tell me where he was, furious that asking him over and over to do it hadn't made a difference, and incensed that I was lying awake when I so desperately wanted to sleep. I imagined him coming home, drunk, and forgetting to lock the door—again.

That night when he came home and I heard his keys dropping on the table, I pushed up from beneath the covers, kicked the socks he had left on the floor, pressed out from the bedroom, and glared at him. He shrugged, and I turned my back on him and slammed the bedroom door. The tap running into the sink and the flush of the toilet turned to footsteps passing by the bedroom door and the squeak of our couch. I woke to an empty bed.

On the train with the German and American couples, the conversation at the brunch table is muted by my worry. I'm distracted now by remembrances of times I wish I had done things differently, and times I wish he had. I let the couples talk, occasionally capturing snapshots of their memories of other trips, an ache spreading like a splash of red paint on my chest. When we go back to our seats, the innate joy of the scene outside my window—all blue skies, trees that are so rich with life they vibrate, and beckoning streams—is too stark a contrast. I bunch my sweater under my head and squish my eyes shut.

There is a hand gently touching my shoulder, and I look around to see that the gray-upholstered seats are half-empty. Up the aisle, as I stand and stretch up on my toes, the golden-haired grandmother looks on, beaming, while her grandson skips ahead. Downstairs, theirs is the only table with space. We sit, just the three of us, waiting for our lunch.

Lacey tells me first about her husband: he's officially retired but not really. He spends most of his days at home in his study. She doesn't know what he's doing in there. Pausing, biting her lower lip, unfocused eyes looking out the window. What does she do, I ask. She volunteers for charities. Of course, there's the weekly family dinners. And then lunch at the club with friends. She's not sure how her hair has held up this long without her hairdresser. This is the first time she's taken her grandson on a trip. Isn't he doing so well? She looks down at him, eyes shining, as he carefully lifts his tea cup to his lips.

She turns the conversation to me, asking about what I do for a living, and where I live. I tell her: "It's beautiful. They call it the city of glass."

Lacey listens to me talk about how people-friendly Vancouver is, how lush with trees and grass. Then she leans forward and lowers her voice.

"Do you have Chinese there?" she asks me, adding a "y" sound in unexpected places, so it comes out "Hayve Chinayse theya?" And when I say yes, and in fact two of my best friends are Chinese, she crinkles her nose, presses back into her chair.

"Do you have Mexicans there?"

"Yes, an old friend of mine is married to a man from Mexico."

"Oh." She recoils again. Shaking her head, she looks up at me from beneath confused and slightly accusatory eyes. "We have them in Alabama, too. And they're takin' our jobs." Oh. In the face of something so blatant, I don't know how to respond. The thing is, she is so childlike. Her soft way of speaking, her confusion about what her husband actually does with his time, her dependence on her grandson to get the waiter's attention when she wants more water. It's as though she's remained sixteen years old, even as her hair lost its depth and her skin went from sun-kissed to sun-spotted.

"I like learning things from my friends who have a different background than mine," I finally say.

I'm thinking of her and how she feels about arriving here as we pull closer to home and I watch the river slide beneath us from the bridge above. Soon we are snaking through warehouses and industrial areas, passing

TV production studios and the docks, finally coming to a stop at the train station. The brass banister is slick beneath my hand as I step down the stairs and onto the platform, where my silver suitcase is waiting for me. And that's all.

Chapter 4

When Joseph bought his first car, he picked me up and drove me into the city, winding down the one-way streets and people-packed intersections to find a restaurant he'd read about. "You're gonna love it. It's French." When we parked, he came around and opened the door. "Let me get it." Taking my hand and guiding me along the sidewalk to the restaurant entrance, where the maître d' smiled as we walked up—two kids playing at being adults—and found Joseph's name on their reservation list. We ate *duck à l'orange* and linguine with scallops and pancetta, baguette warm from the oven, and drank iced tea and lemonade. The candle flame bobbed with our breath, faces drawing closer, our server working around us as he swept the crumbs from the white tablecloth and presented the dessert menu with a flick of his wrist. And when it was time to go—we'd lingered as long as we could—he brought our coats, standing with a repressed smile as he watched Joseph struggle to help me put mine on.

That evening on the way home the rain on the windshield and the roads made the colors all run together like a painting still damp from broad brushstrokes. The music was soft and we drove slowly through the streets, watching women with umbrellas hop over puddles and men in jackets with the collars turned up keep pace. "I don't want to go home," he said, turning to look into my eyes. "I want to keep driving with you all night."

The light turned from green to orange to red and he was still gazing.

"Red light, red light," I shouted.

Brakes squealed and tires dragged, leaving dark black smudges on the pavement, and the other car's wheel cover rolled away, spinning on its edge over and over and over before finally landing on its side, the sounds seeming to arrive in my ear through a thick pallet of foam.

"I'm sorry. I'm so sorry." Joseph was gripping my shoulder. "Are you OK?"

I nodded.

He got out of the car, apologizing to the man who was limping to pick up his wheel cover. "I'm sorry. I'm so sorry." He couldn't stop saying it.

When he got back in the car he was shaking. We drove block after block out of the city and onto the highway and then he was pulling over onto the shoulder and holding his head in his hands. "I never want anything bad to happen to you." We sat in the dark, growing colder, as he folded over himself, until finally the cold was too much and he started the car and pulled out onto the freeway. The rest of the drive home was tentative and careful, Joseph never once going above the speed limit and watching every single light. When he dropped me off—an hour past curfew—he was still apologizing.

At home, the movement of the train still thrumming in my body, I lie on the bed and press my face into Joseph's neck.

When I sit up and look down at him on his back, one arm flung overhead, he looks up at the ceiling.

"What was your past couple of days like?" I ask.

He shrugs. "I went to the pub with Shelly and Keira. Studied some more. Didn't get up to much."

That night I'm awake, thinking about Shelly and Keira. I haven't met them, have just heard about them—two girls he's become friends with. They study together. They're both single, and I can tell by the way he talks about what they ask him about that they like that he does martial arts. I can tell by the way he talks about what they ask him about that he likes that. Whenever Joseph brings them up he doesn't look me in the eye, but squares his shoulders and plants his feet.

Edna laughs when I tell her stories from the train trip, chuckling at my imitation of the grandma from Alabama and the mustached man from Scotland. But then she cuts in: "I've got another assignment for you."

A media coordinator for a tourism board in the prairies has been in touch, inviting an editor from our magazine on a four-day trip this spring—through ranch lands, lake country, and the Head-Smashed-In Buffalo Jump World Heritage Site. It will peak with a night out in the city. "There's one thing you might not like." I wait. "You'll be staying in hotels. Except for the night at Buffalo Jump. You'll be in a tepee." She lifts an eyebrow, the corners of her mouth rising up.

Oh. I nod. Go back to my desk. Read over the e-mail from the media coordinator. A tepee. Me, underneath the stars, at the edge of a cliff, prairie all around, nothing but sky above—and between me and all of that? Nothing but bison hide.

I go back and knock on Edna's door. "I'm a little bit unsure about the whole tepee bit."

Edna looks up from her computer screen, dips her head down, and looks at me over her reading glasses: "You're going."

She's the boss. I'm going. For the rest of the day, I try to look like I'm working. I sit with my fingertips brushing the keyboard, tap about a few nonsensical lines of text whenever someone walks by, take the minimum number of phone calls needed, and mainly just sit and worry. It's not just the tepee part I'm concerned about. I'll be going with a media crew, and we'll share an RV for the daytime part of the trip. My anxiety feeds off long periods of time without space to myself. It grows in the petri dish of other people's personalities—each one broadcasting a different signal, each one coming in at a different vibration, and all of them converging on my senses. Given the choice between an interminably long period of time on my own or an interminably long period of time with other people, I'd choose the solo route. Every time.

I walk home from work. The busloads of people are too much. I turn my face up to the rain and close my eyes, pinpoints of the sky prickling my skin.

Chapter 5

Months later, the day before I'm scheduled to leave, we are eating dinner when I notice a heart inked in black on Joseph's left hand. I freeze, fork hanging suspended in the air and everything else around us fading away, the white cotton curtains I've made growing fuzzy, the fruit on the counter congealing into a mess of color, the artwork on our wall dissolving into space. But the black heart expands, filling my vision, one side bigger than the other, scribbled in with lazy, looping lines.

"What's that?"

Joseph sees where my gaze lands and pulls his hand under the table. A flicker of fear and tension washes across his face.

"Shelly did it. When we were studying."

The image races ahead. Her reaching for his hand, holding it with hers while she colors with the other, head bent over in concentration, hair falling across her face to tickle the top of his arm. What had he done when she'd started? Smiled, laughed, playfully resisted? He hadn't pulled away.

The sound of my chair scraping across the floor brings the surroundings back into sharp relief. I walk into our bedroom, close the door, climb into bed, and pull the covers over my head. I'm lying on my side with my knees pulled up when Joseph comes in; the mattress sinks as he sits down beside me and gently pulls the covers back.

"I don't want to feel like I can't make new friends, just because we're together."

"I've never seen that look on your face before. And, I mean, a heart? On your hand?"

Joseph pauses, looks out the window. "I think you're reacting this way because every time you ask me about them I tense up. They're girls. And I'm friends with them."

"Oh." I don't know what else to say.

The next morning, the Calgary airport is filled with stuffed moose, giant bears in Royal Canadian Mounted Police uniforms, and men who saunter in cowboy boots and hats. The chink, chink, chink of the occasional spur trails behind men in worn-out jeans and hats that have been beaten down by the weather. The slightly acidic smell of strong black coffee is everywhere and overrides the scent of the chamomile tea I hold while waiting for my luggage. After hauling it off the luggage belt, I hail a taxi and watch as six-bedroom homes give way to standard-sized condos and then multi-story apartment buildings and eventually towers.

Despite the repeated vision in the days leading up to the trip of the other media watching in confusion as I kick open the door of the motorhome and sprint away across the prairie, I'm relieved to be away. Away from the reminder of the girls Joseph is hanging out with, the alarm clock that rings out just as I've fallen asleep, and the waves of panic that take me into their undertow multiple times during my workday. I actually feel giddy.

The hotel where I'm meeting the media coordinator and the rest of the journalists who'll be on the trip is short and squat but its lobby is wide and spacious. I've stepped only two feet into it when I'm wrapped in the soft round arms of a woman with great big curly hair. Smoosh. My face meets her cleavage and the scent of Calvin Klein CK One goes straight up my nose.

"Kelly?" My voice comes out muffled.

"You got it." She releases me and steps back. "Glad you made it. Our coach is right over here."

A twenty-four-foot Winnebago sits in the parking lot, driver at the ready, four other people standing around, shifting their weight from side to side.

"We're all here," Kelly smiles, her eyes widening and chin bobbing.

I follow a woman up the stairs and into the Winnebago. She has gray hair that sticks out in all directions, a purple-tinged purse frayed where the buckles sit on the strap, and a notebook held shut with an elastic band. Post-it notes, torn pieces of paper, and newspaper clippings curled and soft at the edges peak out from between the pages.

"I just got back from Japan," she's telling the group. "God, was it tiring. They had us on the most grueling schedule. The only time we were allowed to sleep was on the plane. I was so tired and hungry all the time. One afternoon, we were at lunch with some dignitaries. We'd been up since five in the morning and I was starving. So I'm eating these grapes, and they taste terrible, really bland, but I can't stop myself. I'm in the midst of a conversation with the person to my right when our guide interrupts me: 'Louise, Louise.' I look at him. 'Yes, Gerry.' He lowers his voice: 'You're eating the Styrofoam centerpiece.'"

Kelly laughs, reaching out to pat Louise on the arm.

"We're seeing a lot, but I promise you'll have time to sleep."

The city gives way to the condos and then the sprawling houses on acres of land. Rolling hills peak and ebb. Fence posts race beside us, strung with barbed wire dotted with tufts of hair from the cows standing sullen in the fields. The sky is enormous, a wan empty blue dotted with clouds.

Louise shifts in her seat, pausing in her note-taking to rest her head in her hand and gaze out the window.

"Sometimes I don't even remember what country I'm in. I get off the plane and look for signs."

I smile. "Do you remember where you are today?"

"Oh yes, I always know when I'm home."

An hour later, the sun arcs high into the sky and the Winnebago rumbles its way down a long and curving driveway lined with spruce trees. Flashes of wood buildings and fields of horses appear in the breaks between the leaves, until we pull into a circular driveway leading to a three-story building with white siding and a wide wrap-around porch. Over to one side, the biggest barn I've ever seen sits beaming yellow beneath the sun. In the middle of the drive, a 19th-century five-person carriage with brass fixtures gleams atop a mound of well-coiffed grass.

We are here to see the carriages—all 253 of them.

Soon, we're lined up in three rows on a carriage being pulled by two Clydesdale horses. They're glistening, and even though our driver has told us each horse can comfortably pull our weight, I can't help wondering if they'd rather not. I might be imagining it, but they seem to be looking longingly at the horses nibbling grass, swishing their tails at flies, and every so often arching their necks over to chomp another horse's rear end.

Louise is describing a car rally she drove in Australia, leaning forward in her seat, looking at each one of us and waving her hands around. "I get so confused sometimes about where I am and why. Imagine touching down, jet-lagged after a sixteen-hour flight, and immediately being swept up to the starting-line of a rally.

"There they are, twenty five cars—all gleaming and polished—and already inside one of them is my co-pilot; she's had much more sleep so she's driving. I'm on the map, so I've got it pulled out in front of me. I'm trying to orient us and the gun fires and my co-pilot is off like a shot, but I have no idea where we are.

"So she's pedal to the metal and firing questions at me about where to turn, and I honestly have no idea. I'm still trying to remember what country I'm in. So we get to this roundabout. And we just go round, and round, and round, until she finally careens right and we're bee-lining down a straightaway and I'm feeling really proud because I think I've just figured out where we are. And I'm right. We're back at the starting line. And the announcer is saying 'And here comes the Mazda, again.'"

We're all nodding and laughing and agreeing, each one of us adding that we're hopeless with directions, too, which makes me wonder two things: one, is being hopeless with directions something that most writer-media types have in common? And two, if it is something most writer-media types have in common, who on earth ever thought it was a good idea to continually send us to places where we've never been? Suddenly I have a picture of countries of astonishing beauty and rich cultural treasures being wandered about in by confused, lost men and women with notepads, taking notes like mad and walking quickly and purposefully, but always in circles.

Thankfully, we have Kelly. And she herds us back onto the motor home, handing out snacks and drinks. When Jim, the sole male in our crew other than our driver, decides to take a nap, I realize that we are, in a way, like kindergartners. Here we are, naive in our lack of knowledge about the subject, being handed out sound bite–sized tidbits of information in an always-entertaining way, never having to decide where to go or what to do next, and being given breaks for snacks and naps. When Louise asks Kelly if she can have another juice box, I realize we've all consciously given up our adulthood—at least for the moment.

While Louise drinks her grape juice, I give myself over to the worry that's been at me since I boarded the plane. I am convinced that something bad is going to happen to me in that tepee. Surely, in the middle of the rolling hills, with nothing around, not even another person, for miles and miles, lying by myself wrapped up in my sleeping bag like an enchilada, something is going to get me. What something? I don't know. I've never been to southern Alberta, but my imagination can conjure up at least three things that are scary. One, an enraged bison, en route with his herd to their usual gathering place, annoyed at me for planting a tepee there right in his way. He tramples me before I can even squeak out that I didn't want to be there in the first place. Two, whatever it is that hunts buffalos. Surely they have some kind of predator, and if it can take down a bison, it can take down an already prone Lindsey. Three, a gun-toting rogue cowboy; he has wild hair sticking out on all angles and a giant—yes, giant—gray beard stained with chewing tobacco. And I have no idea why he's mad, I just know he is, and when he stomps into my tepee I'm already trying to climb one of the poles up and out the smoke-hole.

I notice Louise has finished her grape juice and has her eyes closed. She looks calm.

"Louise, have you ever slept in a tepee?" One eye cracks open as Louise squints and considers me, and, I think, the question. "It's just that I'm a little worried . . ." The other eye cracks open. The rest of it all comes out in a rush: "About being stomped on by a bison or eaten by whatever eats them or shot by a rogue cowboy."

"Lindsey—" says the woman who has trekked through jungles in the Amazon and navigated a single-engine boat through crocodile-infested waters in Louisiana, "seriously." Then she smiles, shakes her head, nods—*that's final*—before folding her extra sweater up for a pillow, turning away with a sigh, and closing her eyes.

Louise is still calm when we're setting up camp for the night. The tepees are in a circle, poles arranged to support the hide, which is painted white with polka dots and images of bison. Beyond the tepees is short, prickly prairie grass, and beyond all that are the cliffs. Which is where, just as the name says, the bison jumped and had their head smashed in—at the Head-Smashed-In Buffalo Jump World Heritage Site.

Our tepees aren't where they actually would have been, which is down in the valley where First Nations people gathered to process that influx of supply for food, tools, and materials. We're up on the flat land leading up to the cliffs . . . which, of course, I'm loving, given that, even though I am nowhere near close to being a bison, I'm convinced somebody will try to herd us over. If the bison predators or rogue cowboy or angry bison don't get us first.

Kelly isn't concerned at all. She's done this before. We're the third group she's taken on a tour and spent the night with in a tepee. As soon as she mentioned she'd done this before and I spotted how absolutely unconcerned she was about it all I began to stick to her, never letting her out of my sight until the moment when she started assigning tepees and asked who'd like to bunk with her and I started waving my hand around even though I was standing two inches away. "Lindsey? You wanna bunk with me?"

"Oh, me? I never thought of it until now."

She's brought us all sleeping bags that are the latest in heat retention and lightness, and down pillows and extra thermal blankets to lay on top of the extra-wide air mattresses—all of which, of course, is historically accurate. When I tell her I often wake up to eat a snack in the middle of the night, she just laughs.

"That's fine with me."

We're lying on opposite sides of the tepee, and through the smoke-hole I can see the moon.

"Hey, Kelly?"

"Yeah."

"Do you like your job?"

"Don't you?"

"Well, I do—I think I do. It's just that I'm not sure about how to do all the other stuff. I'm not sure how to do my job and keep my relationship healthy, and me healthy, and everybody happy—all at the same time."

"Lindsey," she raises herself up on one elbow and I can feel her looking at me through the dark, "You don't have to do it all perfectly."

Up through the smoke-hole, past the museum and the occasional cloud is a sky full of stars. And beyond that are more stars, and more galaxies, and more moons and suns and planets. And for some reason that's beyond me, I have the soundest sleep I've had in weeks.

In the morning, I unroll my yoga mat overlooking the canyon and sit very still—just listening. The breeze is blowing and the grass is whispering, wave after wave of soft sighs rising from the earth. A bird calls overhead. And there are moments in between the sounds of the grass and the call of the birds where there's nothing, where there's silence that stretches up to meet the sky. In those moments I feel a silence within me, too, a kind of silence that feels quieter than any lack of sound, a stillness that is deep and constant.

Which is the opposite of what I'm feeling later that day as I straddle a giant gray horse named Jed. Jed is a tall horse. He's got a thick, dark mane and deep brown eyes with long lashes. When I first slung my leg across the saddle, he turned back to look at me, blinking slowly, chewing a long piece of grass. He's also slow, padding one foot after the other, bringing up the rear of the line of eight horses our group is riding, with one guide in front, one in back, and all of our tour crew together in the middle. Every time I get to ride a horse in a group, I get the one that plods slowly at the back of the line. Since I know that horse tour companies always try to match the horse with the rider, to choose the person and horse that suit each other best—well, I try not to think too much about that.

"Give him a good kick, Lindsey." This directive comes from the cowboy I was afraid would appear in the middle of the night, except that instead of appearing in the middle of the night he's appeared in the middle of the day, as one of our guides for the ride at the ranch. He has wild hair sticking out on all angles and a giant—yes, giant—gray beard stained with chewing tobacco. His legs are bowed. And I have no idea why he's angry, I just know he is. "Git goin' Jed," he says—and just like that, too.

I don't want to kick Jed. I don't want the cowboy to tap him on the rump with his whip, either. Jed seems to me to be doing just fine, carefully and cautiously picking his way down a creek full of loose rocks. It occurs to me that Jed probably knows exactly what pace will work best for him in order to navigate the slippery rocks and steep slope, and that he might even know exactly what will happen if he goes faster: he'll lose his rider. Which, come to think of it, he might not mind at all, given that she's clearly unskilled when it comes to being on a horse's back, what with all the non-graceful thumping and whumping happening up there. But still, Jed continues to go slowly, carefully, even gingerly.

Our guide winds us through a valley strung with poplar and birch trees, pointing to an eagle as it arcs overhead above the trees. We follow it up and out to the top of the hills, where from our perch we can see the valley we've just climbed out of, green hillsides sloping down, creek winding through, trees linking leaves to form a canopy where birds call to each other. The sky above is the color of skies in children's books. Even the angry cowboy becomes calmer and sits back a little on his horse, arms folded across his chest, face softening.

All of us are complaining of aching bums and legs when we get back to the ranch and finally climb down off our horses. Jed gets a carrot from me, which he accepts with soft, whiskery lips from the palm of my hand. I watch him as he's led back to the stable by a farmhand, tail swishing flies away, chewing methodically. Dinner will be hay, and he'll be washed down with a hose.

That evening, we arrive at our own watering hole, a five-star prairie resort run by a national hotel chain. The marketing director is hosting us in a private room at the restaurant. She's the tall, short-haired woman wearing a man's button-up shirt and pressed black pants who stood on the driveway waving as we pulled in. She had our luggage taken to our rooms and walked us around the property. Now she's sitting beside me at the massive table beneath a rack of antlers, saying something about the food. I've stopped paying attention. I'm listening to my heart starting to beat faster and feeling my neck being squeezed. There's that faint ringing sound in my head.

I'm trying to shake it off, to think of something else. But I can't. I need to go. I need to get away from here. I am shovelling a last bite of dinner and standing up, pushing my chair away from the table with the backs of my legs. I am arranging the corners of my mouth into the edges of a smile and speaking through clenched teeth. I am ignoring the baffled look on Kelly's face as I turn my back on all of that noise, too much noise, and head for the nearest doorway out.

Down the hall, left turn, up the stairs and slide the key into the lock. Closing the door behind me, feeling its smooth coolness against my back. Feeling the grip around my neck release.

Chapter 6

One day not so long before the first of these trips Joseph and I were eating lunch in the sun. He wanted to watch a documentary that night, an in-depth look at lions and their mating, sleeping, and hunting habits. But the thought of watching antelope being hunted and eaten makes me recoil.

"What?" he said. "It's natural." I shrugged, biting my lip. "You don't like watching them being hunted down?" Pausing for effect, and then: "The little ones or the weaker ones falling behind, almost getting away, starting to panic as they realize they're being left behind. And then getting caught, in terror, their necks being snapped—why are you crying?"

Minutes later the bench shifted as he sat beside me and laid his hand on my back. "I'm sorry. I don't know why I did that."

I do. Something is seeping into the cracks in our relationship. And it's coming from both of us.

Pictures of me as a young girl show me with dark circles under my eyes. "From worrying too much," my mom would tell me. As a kid I often woke up terrified that something was coming for me—whether it was the man with bony fingers under the bed, the witch from a play we'd seen weeks before about to fly through the window, or a man in a black toque casting an oversize shadow as he crept down the hallway toward my bedroom. I'd gather all of the courage I had, stand up on the edge of my bed, and then leap as far away from what was surely underneath it as I could. I'd land and then squint my eyes against whatever was coming down the hall and race across into my parent's bedroom. Many nights, my dad decamped to sleep in my room while I tucked myself into my mom's arm.

Anxiety causes you to look for the source. Even as a kid, you're aware that something is wrong. And until somebody can tell you otherwise, you believe it's outside you. You just know that something terrible is coming that you need to be worried about. But you don't know what. You don't know when. And you have no idea how to prepare. As an adult, control seems to be the most logical antidote. *If I don't know what to prepare for, I'll prepare for everything.* I never miss a deadline. I'm always able to update Edna on every project I'm in charge of and tell her the details of the next steps. I'm on top of whatever I do, and I do a better job than is asked of me.

I never wake up without feeling like somebody's hands are around my throat.

At the office, an incoming phone call makes my head spin, the ringing sound mimicked by the dizzying ringing in my head that comes along with the panic response. Every time Brian surprises me by starting to talk to me while strolling into my office while my back is turned, the rush of blood to my head makes my vision turn red. On my employee review was the comment, "Lindsey gets stressed when she's not in control." Edna gave a shrug and replied "Who doesn't?"

Every day, I fight a losing battle. I cling to routine like a drowning woman to a life ring—except that it never pulls me up and out of the churning waters; it just keeps me afloat and always in the same spot. When Joseph wants to watch the fireworks on the beach, the closing sensation in my throat and the lack of breath cause me to physically recoil. I immediately imagine myself consumed by anxiety the next day, unable to make it through one minute without the hands getting tighter and tighter around my neck. I wait until it's too late to say yes and then say no. Joseph glares at me and then stomps into the study to play video games.

When his friends come by to pick him up for tae kwon do, I duck into the living room to avoid them, drained from a day spent riding the roller coaster of highs and lows of extreme anxiety and total deflation.

Anxiety is like the abusive man I saw once walking down the sidewalk with the girl who stayed with him in spite of it. He had her hoodie gathered in a knot behind her head and was twisting it tighter as he pushed her forward. Her hands pulling against the fabric in a desperate attempt to stop it from cutting off her breath, she was trying to make light of it, trying to make it into a joke. He kicked at her feet, making her walk and tripping her at the same time. She held fast to the fabric, laughing in a way that sounded like crying, panic in her eyes.

I'd do nearly anything to stop this feeling.

One morning over breakfast Joseph asked if we could do something different with the blankets on our bed.

"There are so many blankets between us that when I try to cuddle you I can't even get close and just end up holding your hand."

"I do that on purpose."

He recoiled, hunching forward as though he'd been hit in the stomach. I kept eating. I won't say it was kind. I will say that when you're on day 342 of nearly no sleep, you can in some moments become somebody very hard to love. I haven't slept well since we moved in together, lying awake at night willing myself to be able to stop sensing his every breath. Willing myself to release enough of the tension in my body to drift away into sweet relief.

When I do sleep, I drop deep into it, flat on my back with both arms flung above my head, my body finally succumbing to rest. I snore. Joseph complains in the morning, looking at me suspiciously as though I've become someone he doesn't recognize: "You snore really loud."

One night I wake up to a sharp pain in my upper arm that makes me gasp and sit up to rub away the sensation. The next morning I tell Joseph about it: "It was so strange. It really hurt." Joseph's face tightens and he bites his lip as he looks away. "Oh, that's weird."

Later in the day I realize that the look on his face, the one I'd seen only once before and had wondered about for hours afterward, was guilt. Overcome with tiredness himself, stressed and angry, he'd pinched me hard to stop me from snoring.

We had talked about marriage. Not endlessly, in the way couples who are in love and earnestly planning the future do, but sporadically and heatedly. He wanted to. I didn't. One evening we go to a commitment ceremony together. Having found each other later in life, his cousin and the man she fell in love with had decided to forgo the wedding, but keep the intention. We watch from plastic chairs as they face each other and talk about how much they love one another, how thankful they are to have finally found the person they'd been waiting for. In the car on the way home, as we drive carefully down a winding road in the dark, Joseph quietly asks, "What about a commitment ceremony? Would you be OK with that?"

I look away. "I'll think about it."

Caught in the lock box of my own mind, I miss the snap of the final thread that's been pulled too tight, and the small sigh of surrender as the fabric that wove us together settles in two pieces.

Chapter 7

I'm walking down the sidewalk carrying bags full of produce and milk, hot from the summer sun and constant adrenaline surges, when I send up a silent prayer: "Grocery shopping shouldn't be this hard. I really, really need help. Please." The next thing I notice is a sign on the door of a herbal dispensary: "Ayurvedic consultations. Inquire inside."

One of my best friends from high school had told me about Ayurveda, the ancient Indian health system. Anna meditated and did an asana practice nearly every morning, and although she never dieted, what she ate was dictated by what she'd learned was good for her Ayurvedic constitution. She'd told me some things about what would be good for me, and encouraged me to learn how to take care of my health by eating and meditating. I was fascinated, but never really listened.

But a sign is a sign.

The smell of incense is the first thing I notice when I arrive that Saturday to meet my new doctor. Dressed in a crisp new suit, with cufflinks and tie that matches his turban, Dr. Ayer hands me a questionnaire and brings me tea. "This," he tells me after reading my responses, "tells me how you are out of balance. My goal is get you back into balance. So you feel better." He places two fingers on my pulse and closes his eyes. "You have a Vata imbalance, and a bit too much Pitta. Do you have a hard time sleeping?"

"Yes."

"Do you wake up about four in the morning?"

"Yes."

"Do your hands and feet often feel cold and do you have a hard time staying warm?"

"Yes."

"Does your mind feel like it's always spinning?"

"How do you know?"

"I'm going to prescribe some lifestyle changes and give you some suggestions on what to eat, to help you feel better."

I wouldn't have cared if he'd asked me to eat beetle dung and bathe in cow's milk. After multiple visits to my family doctor as a teen, complaining of my racing heart and how I always felt anxious, only to be met with tests that yielded no diagnosis and so no suggestions for what I could do, I wanted to cry with relief. Finally, somebody who understood. Somebody who could help.

The first thing my new doctor prescribes is a morning yoga routine. It's about thirty minutes long, and involves simple sun salutations and a seated posture I'm to stay in for five minutes while thinking about things I'm grateful for. The second thing is to eat less sugar, more protein, and more moist, warm, oily foods. No toast. No crackers. No roasted nuts. No popcorn. Chocolate is out.

I am in.

One morning, weeks after beginning my new lifestyle, I wake up without the feeling of hands squeezing tighter around my neck. I can breathe. No, I am being breathed. The inhales and the exhales fill me and empty me, an ocean of breath washing my worries away. Instead of my mind immediately transporting me into the office and everything I need to accomplish that day, I simply lie in bed. I feel the blanket snug around my body. I feel the sheets on my skin. I see the sun streaming through the window, the dust motes dancing on the air. I notice I feel hungry. I get up. Pad into the kitchen. Stand at the counter and eat an orange. Then I get ready for my day.

Outside, it is a brand new world. How had I never noticed the color of the trees outside our door? When had the daffodils bloomed? I see everything; it feels like the first time.

When anxiety has a hold on you, your vision narrows. You don't see what's around you, because you're focused on the threat—even if there really isn't one. I'd spent most of my life this way. As a kid, when we went for walks in the woods as a family, I'd refuse to be anywhere other than with Dad in front and Mom in the back. I wanted to be right between them, so I'd be safe. I spent most of the walk focusing on Dad's back. The same narrow vision had accompanied me all my life—and I had never known it.

Now, walking down the sidewalk is like being in a movie. Look at that bird singing on the tree branch. See how the camera pans to the base of the tree where a fat gray squirrel sits clinging to the bark. Watch now as we slide eastward and see a white-haired Greek man with gnarled fingers argue good-naturedly with the man he's buying his bread from. And then, the lineup of characters at the bus: the woman with her dance shoes peeking out from her black leather work-bag; the teenager with his headphones in and his collar turned up; the man with coiffed hair carrying an umbrella.

This is a whole new world.

As the weeks pass, I begin choosing yoga class over opening night at the theatre, clothing line launches, the tasting-debut of new menu items by the hottest chefs, and club and restaurant openings. Edna, Eileen, and Sofie—the editor directly above me in the hierarchy—tell me the next day about everything I'd missed: the food, the pretty people, the drama, the free clothes and gift certificates, the invitation to next week's event. One day, Sofie tells me in the midst of it all the previous evening she'd turned to Edna and said, "Lindsey'll be sorry she missed this." But nothing feels better than the new world I'm living in, and nothing is worth sacrificing it for. I don't feel like I'm missing a thing; I feel like I'm gaining everything.

Joseph is frustrated. He doesn't understand why I'm asking him to gather his stuff from the living room the night before so I can begin my day there in private—just me and my yoga practice. He finds it confusing that

I want to sit silently for five minutes after dinner, instead of doing something else.

He complains that my twice-a-week evening yoga classes land on days he is home, instead of days when he's out doing his martial arts training: "We never see each other; we live like roommates. Aren't there other yoga classes you can go to?"

Thrilled with how I feel, I am waking up in the morning humming, pulling open the curtains, letting in the light. Joseph asks me if I can hold off on the humming until after he's had his breakfast.

Chapter 8

She is calling from the entrance to the living room: "I hope you feel better soon." I'm lying sick on the couch, piles of used Kleenex on the floor beside me, throat raw, set to watch reruns of *Sex and the City*, and Joseph is going out with his martial arts crew. He's told me about a girl named Kerri who recently joined the class. She is an easy going East Coaster with auburn hair and a freckled nose, a lover of surfing, big dogs, and traveling to unexpected places. She has just broken up with her long-term boyfriend.

In her voice as she calls out to me across the apartment I hear something other than a woman being kind, which she is. I hear the voice of someone who is like me—only better.

He loves her. I know. Instantly.

I also know he hasn't admitted it to himself.

A few weeks later, I tell Joseph I've booked a week of vacation. "Where are we going?" he asks. I tell him I'm going alone.

I drive for ten hours. Through the Rocky Mountains, past lakes and truck-stop pull-outs, through small towns that end nearly as soon as they begin. Straight out to the Kootenays, to the place my family went to every summer when I was a child.

My grandparents had both died three years before. First, my Grandpa, of a stroke that left him alive for just a few days afterward, with hollow cheeks and sunken eyes. And then, days later, my Grandma. When my aunt found her, she lay crumpled on the floor, a shell in Grandma's hand-knitted sweater, polyester pants, and white running shoes. Her friends said it was a broken heart. It made sense to me. He had aged ungracefully, and she'd spent her last years caring for him, short-tempered and frustrated with his inability to do simple things for himself: get water in the middle of the night, go to the bathroom, bathe. But when he died, she had wandered their house aimlessly, moving heavily from the back to the front, and back again, crying silent tears as she picked things up and put them down. I hadn't been back since they died. We didn't gather as a family anymore. The anchors on the ship were gone.

As I drive up the dirt road toward my grandparents' old home, it all comes flooding back. Endless summer days spent playing sardines under the peach trees with my sister and cousins. Climbing on the roof of Grandpa's garage, to sit hidden from the others and watch and listen. Tucked in between the young trees that formed a circle up behind the shed, where no one would find me, eating raspberries and reading.

All eight of us cousins would eat cherries sitting in a circle on Grandma's back porch, stringing pairs of them over our ears, letting them dangle like earrings that Miss Chiquita might wear. As often as our parents would take us, we'd make the hour-long drive down to the lake and pile out of the cars at Uncle Joe's place. A good friend of Grandpa's, he wasn't technically an uncle but had been around for so long he'd become family. Never married, he lived alone on the edge of the lake, chasing the local kids off his property.

When we arrived he would come out from the house with a small smile, carrying chips three years past their expiration date and hard marshmallows. We'd spend the day on the dock, reading comic books until we got hot. Then we'd jump in the lake, turning and spiralling, climbing on logs floating on the surface and falling off them again. Sometimes, if we were lucky, Uncle Joe took us out in his boat, pointing out an eagle's nest or a spot where the loon dove deep the last time he'd seen it. At the end of the day, waving goodbye to him as we drove away, we'd see him wipe tears from the corners of his eyes.

If we couldn't convince our parents to take us to the lake, we went to the pool. Grandma's friend Mrs. T would have the cover pulled back, the pool noodles laid out, and the inflatables blown up. We practiced our dives, Grandma sitting on the sidelines with Mrs. T, giving directions: "Straighten your arms a bit more. Less bend to your knees. Too much splash." Afterward, Grandma would pull into the Dairy Queen at the bottom of the hill and order ice cream for us at the drive-through window.

We ate it silently, the wetness of our bathing suits seeping into the towels Grandma had us lay on the seat.

This was my safe place. Around every corner was somebody who loved you. And although they were unique in their own ways, my mom's three sisters were enough like her that it was like having four different versions of her nearby. My Aunt Jen and Uncle Greg had moved back to the Kootenays from Toronto when they had their first child. They wanted their kids to grow up knowing their grandparents, so she and Uncle Greg built a house on the land right beside my grandparents' and started a soap-making company at the other end of town.

It's Aunt Jen's door I knock on when I arrive. Tunic grazing her ankles, golden retriever tucked behind her legs, Aunt Jen pulls me into a hug, soft cheek pressing for a moment against mine. The house smells of fresh bread. Later, at dinner, where she has laid out sliced tomatoes and cucumbers from her garden and sprinkled them with salt and pepper like Grandpa used to do, Aunt Jen asks me how I'd like to spend my week. I've been picturing it the whole drive. And when I tell her, she grins.

We fill that week with lazy, country summer days. We swim in the river, letting it carry us downstream until we decide to clamber out. We drive down to the lake and sit with our books on the rocky beach until we are warm enough to brave the glacier-fed waters that felt much warmer when I was seven. I ride a bike down to the main street to poke through the bookstores I loved as a teen. And climb a tree barefoot outside the high school, where I sit tucked up in the branches until I feel my legs fall asleep. I wander over to the house my grandparents built and lie down on the grass to cry.

I spend hours sitting in a hammock on the front porch overlooking the valley. The stars at night are endless. Often as I sit out there I spot a shooting star racing across the sky, plummeting from its orbit in a grand-finale exit. I wonder how the grand-finale exit will go for me and Joseph. Will we arc gracefully from the place that we've been, to land somewhere new and look around in wonder? Or will we burn up everything that we have?

Joseph doesn't reply to any of the e-mails I send him.

The evening I get home, my "Hello" rings out in the empty apartment. There's a note on the kitchen table: "I'm out with Alec."

I remember a moment from our last trip together, the road trip through the middle of British Columbia, camping and driving, driving and camping. One day, when we were close enough to a major center to catch a radio signal, a Jack Johnson song came on: "Must I always keep waiting, waiting on you? I can't always keep playing, playing the fool." Joseph turned up the volume: "I love this song."

When he gets home that night, I curl onto the bed and blurt out, "I can't do this anymore." He is calm and peaceful, rubbing my back and apologizing for not being upset. "It's just, I mean, it's not like it really changes things. I'll always love you."

Chapter 9

I leave first, having spent the three weeks after our breakup trekking each block between our apartment and the office in the rain of early fall, knocking on apartment building doors, giving my name to building managers, asking to be put on their waiting list. Hoping that when they received notice that someone was leaving I would be the first person they would call. Each night, we still slept in the same bed, me quietly sobbing into the blankets. After the first night, when he told me he was sorry but he couldn't be the one to comfort me, Joseph lay silent and stiff on the other side of the bed until I stopped.

The apartment I find is tiny. A studio in a three-story walk-up built in the 1920s, it has two windows, a bed in a giant drawer that pulls out from under a walk-in closet, and a kitchen for one. The oven is too small for a standard-sized baking sheet. The bar fridge is too small to hold a week's shopping. From the outside, the building is all creamy tones and elegantly curving lines—classic and statuesque. Inside, it's worn and dirty, with a front entrance layered with dust and footprints.

It isn't cozy, it isn't tidy, and it doesn't feel like home. But I can't keep waking up with the pain of Joseph beside me but not with me. I can't keep making breakfast in silence, and wondering where he is when he doesn't get home until after midnight. So I pay the damage deposit, the first month's rent, and half the rent for the remaining two months on our old place. I pack up as fast as I can, collecting all of my things in cardboard boxes that begin to fill our living room.

I move most of them by myself, in stages, remembering how different it had been the last time I'd been transporting boxes from one place to another after a long day of work. We were happy and excited, thrilled with our new place and the relatively low rent. Thrilled to be in a neighborhood known for its tree-lined streets, hip young families, and active, healthy lifestyle.

My new neighborhood is more stylish, less family-oriented, and pricier. Shops on its main street are the ones we include in the magazine when we're talking about high-end places to shop. If an independently owned boutique with lower prices tries to make it, we soon see its windows shuttered by cardboard. It's quickly replaced by an opulent chain. When I write about the neighborhood for the magazine, I inevitably use the adjective "tony."

Like in many cities, living in a tony neighborhood in Vancouver means living in a tiny place, for a rent that astounds people who live only thirty minutes away. And it doesn't mean your tiny home is in line with the quality of the shops around you. I can hear each step down the hallway, and every creak of the stairs. My neighbor across the hall has detailed conversations with her girlfriends about the last guy she had sex with. I hear about them all. And across the courtyard, the couple who both work nights at clubs downtown fight constantly. He yells and throws furniture; she pleads and cries.

Days after I move in, I come home to find my front door wide open. I call the building manager in a panic. He responds without a trace of worry or apology: "That must have been from when we were in there with the fire alarm testing company." He is unconcerned. I'm the opposite. There is no knowing that when I lock the door it will stay that way, no certainty that nobody but me will enter my home, no knowing everything will be OK. That night, I begin a new habit: moving a dresser in front of my door before I go to bed.

There are silverfish everywhere—a slippery kind of bug that hides when you turn on the light and plagues older buildings. The day they are being fumigated I escape to the one place I can think of: Joseph's place. He's moved into the building he wanted to live in when we first moved in together: an airy, windowed studio with soundproof cement walls. I sit on the one piece of furniture he has, his bed, and daydream about living there.

That night, I wake up in my own single bed, bones rattling. Beneath me bass, electric guitar and drums are rising through the floor. I scramble for my alarm clock. Midnight on a Tuesday. Ear plugs. Where are they? The third drawer. I stuff them in my ears, wrap a scarf around my head, and bury beneath the pillow. The bass is persistent, though, and worms into my head. The next night, it happens again. And then two nights after that.

I begin making lines on two sheets of paper—one for nights with music, one for nights without. The with-music sheet is soon black with lines. I'm not sure why I'm doing this, I don't know who will care if I show it to them, and just looking at it makes my heart start to pound. But I keep making more lines.

It's New York that keeps me from collapsing. In movies, my heroes are young women who set out on their own in the Big Apple. They live in places the size of a closet, on streets lined with graffiti. They hang their laundry from the fire escape and order takeout because they have no oven or stove. They face down burly construction workers, neighbors knocking on their door—drunk and grasping—and the occasional rat. What keeps them going is a dream.

If they can do it, so can I. I hang drapes and artwork, make curtains to pull around my bed, and spend weeks sourcing perfect ways to save space. The white metal radiator, kitchen large enough to fit only a bar fridge, and enormous walk-in closet that takes up one-third of the apartment actually bring me joy—it's like in the movies.

The midnight band practices stay. I am useless at confrontation. I call the building manager for help, and he shows up once or twice to tell the guy below me to turn it down. I write notes begging him to stop, which I slide under his door when I'm sure he is out. Multiple times a week, electric guitars and drums blast through my already haphazard sleep. My anxiety gets worse. I feel like I am always trembling.

What saves me is the yoga studio. I can show up stressed, nervous, tense, and angry and sit down on the mat and not talk to anyone. I can arrive weighed down by memories and carrying the hole in my chest and the people waiting for the class to start will smile, ask questions, and make conversation; the hole gets smaller. When dinnertime for me is band practice for the guy downstairs and I begin to feel like panic will shatter me, I grab my mat and run for the door.

Two months after I move in, I meet Joseph for coffee. He's e-mailed me to ask if I want to meet up, just to catch up. But there is something that makes me feel I need to prepare myself before I get there; he is going to tell me something that will be hard to hear. When I arrive, he's sitting at the counter on a tall stool, staring into his cup. "Oh, hey," he smiles, getting up to give me a hug. I hold on longer than a friend should, and he lets me bury my face in his neck. He smells just the way I remember.

There's so much to tell him—I've even brought my laptop to show him a clip of me on TV, talking about holiday gifts for hostesses. He is disgusted that I'd called a vacuum cleaner sexy. It had been easier to talk about than the pair of cufflinks: one decorated with the image of a rooster and the other with the image of a cat.

During the first pause in the conversation, Joseph blurts out, "Your dad sent me a birthday card, with a gift. Why did he do that?" He is upset, shifting constantly on his stool.

"Um. Because he's nice that way?"

"But we're not together anymore."

"He just cares about you, Joseph. You were a part of our family."

"Does he think we're getting back together?"

"No. He doesn't think that."

Joseph takes a deep breath, looks out the window and exhales slowly. When he looks back at me there are tears in his eyes.

"I have to tell you something."

This is it. I know what comes next.

"Ok. It's OK. Really. Just give me one second. I need to go to the bathroom."

In the bathroom I stand with my hands on the sides of the sink, looking at myself. How do I want to respond? I weigh my choices. Raging and crying would be honest. But it wouldn't be fair. And it wouldn't help us stay friends. I've contributed to this moment, too. So I imagine myself being kind. Understanding. Accepting. And I stand in that bathroom until I can actually see myself doing it.

When I sit back down beside him, I give him a small smile, encouraging him to say it.

"I'm seeing someone." I nod. "It's Kerri, from my martial arts class." I nod again. "I'm sorry." There is a tear making a steady path down his cheek. "When I said I'd always . . . care for you . . . I meant it."

I make the words come out: "It's OK. You and I have been growing apart for a long time now."

He is relieved. "I know. That's what I told Kerri. I mean, she just broke up with her boyfriend of five years, and we were talking about what people would think, but the two of them were in the same boat as you and I were. And I can't keep on keeping her a secret from you. It's not fair to you, and it's not fair to her. She's really great. I think you'd like her."

I bite my lip, swallow down the lump in my throat. Squeeze my eyes shut against the tears. When I open them again he is searching my face.

"Will you walk me to the bus stop?"

"Sure," he says, his face softening and shoulders releasing.

He stands in the cold with me until I'm on the bus, and I wave goodbye through the window, watching as he grows smaller.

Back at home in my tiny apartment, I wrap myself in a blanket and look around at what I have left. A desk. Two shelves. A kitchen table that folds away so I can pull my bed out from the wall. Some pictures. Drapes. A too-big closet. And me. Just me. For the first time in seven years.

Below me, the electric guitars and drums start up. The pictures on my walls begin to vibrate. So does the chair I am sitting on. I begin to feel the familiar sensation of panic, and the slow, steady pressure of hands around my neck. My heart pounds in my ears and I begin seeing everything through a curtain of red.

God damn, I am tired of feeling this way.

Night after night for weeks before I had decided to make the trip out to the Kootenays, I'd had a recurring dream. In it I sat on the edge of Kootenay Lake on the beach we'd loved as kids. Beside me sat me at seven years old. She is tiny, skinny arms wrapped around knees drawn up to her chin and tears trickling down her cheeks. She points at the skyline—a city looming high over the edge of the trees. Slowly and steadily the skyscrapers are coming closer, covering everything in their path. She looks at me with sad, confused eyes: "You let them in."

She is the part of me I've methodically denied as I molded myself into a magazine editor, the successful daughter, and the very picture of a young woman on the rise. She is the part of me that actually dreads going to evening events. The part of me that kept asking "But what about Paris? You said we'd go to Paris," each time I talked about New York. She is the part of me that feels calm.

In the car on the way to Aunt Jen's, she sat beside me on the passenger seat—happily bouncing her feet to the music, looking ahead around every corner. Taking her with me to the Kootenays was just the beginning. I am going to get her back for good.

Chapter 10

I've been holding my arms stretched out in front of me at a sixty-degree angle for twenty-five minutes now. They're beginning to shake. My shoulders hurt. My neck is tensing up. I am furious. Our teacher for the rest of the yoga workshop is up on stage. She looks elated. "Keep going. Keep up and you'll be kept up. Don't give up." I love her, but . . . I hate her.

My lower back is starting to ache, my hips went numb ten minutes ago, and my ankles feel bruised. I'm thinking of giving up. I'm thinking about what it would feel like to lower my arms, lie down on my back, and close my eyes. I'm picturing the sweet relief of doing nothing. "Keep going," she chants. "Keep up and you'll be kept up." Dammit. I've paid for this experience. Not only this one, but three hours of experiences just like it. I'm starting to think about what else I could be doing today. Namely, nothing. Oh, sweet relief.

And then, there is nothing.

Rather, suddenly I'm gone. It's as though I've left my body. I just don't feel it anymore. No pain.

No discomfort. No aches. I check to see if I lay down without noticing it. Nope. Same position. I check to see if I lowered my arms without noticing it. Nope. Same position. What's happened to what I was feeling? What's happened to, well, everything?

Because nothing feels the same anymore. Nothing.

I'm still in the same position, still in the room, still at this workshop, and yet—I'm not. I'm immersed in something wondrous. I'm being held by an incredible force. I'm being loved more deeply and more intensely than I ever have been before. There's joy. There's delight. And something else. It's like the force that is loving me is also kind of laughing at me. Kind of saying, "Oh, you lovely funny bumbling you."

I'm looking behind me to see if someone has come up and started hugging me. No one's there. But I'm being *held*. I'm being cradled. Every cell in my body is immersed in this love-bath that silently, steadily, and firmly communicates: I love you for all that you are. Every single bit of you. I love you for who you've been, what you've done, and where you've been. I love you for the moments you made your biggest mistakes, the times you were selfish and mean. I love you for the jealousy and the insecurities. I love all of you. I love you for all that you are.

There are tears streaming down my cheeks. I can't stop them.

And then I begin to apologize. I'm praying out "I'm sorry's"—not for what I've done, but for what I will do. I conjure up every person in my life who I think will be disappointed by what will happen next, who might be afraid of how my future will turn out. I see my dear, responsible dad in all his fear and worry and I say, "Dad, I'm sorry. I just can't do this anymore." I see my patient, loving mom in all her hope and concern and I say, "Mom, I'm sorry. I just can't do this anymore." I see a crowd of people getting larger by the minute: elementary school teachers, high school teachers, neighbors, and friends' parents. Everyone who ever told me, "This is what I see in you. And this is what I think you can be." And I say, "I'm sorry."

I'm sorry.

Because I'm letting it go. I'm letting go of the person I thought I should be. The person they thought I should be. I have no idea—no idea!—who I will become or how I will get there. I just know a part of me feels absolutely still. Absolutely calm. And absolutely certain. That part of me feels no anxiety. That part of me is in absolute peace.

And I think God just told her that's the way it can always be. That's the way it's meant to be.

A few weeks before, Iairos had joined me on the bench overlooking False Creek. He sat looking out at the water, watching the rainbow-colored ferries trail a gentle wake behind them. The sailboats with their sails curled in and people chatting on the deck. We were silent.

When he spoke, he didn't turn his head but kept his eyes on an orange kayak nosing the edge of the water.

"You seem sad today."

I hadn't slept. Had experienced another surge of red when a colleague knocked on my door and . . . I ached. The ache was like a moss that had crept up slowly onto my skin, had knit itself together over my surface. It was hard to move; each time I lifted a limb to find freedom, the moss simply regrew, getting denser.

"I'm so tired, Iairos." I turned to look at him. He had heard me say this before, had begun to be a witness to my inner landscape and the gaping hole I found there.

He nodded. Patted my hand. Watched the kayak grow smaller in the distance.

"Do what makes you happy. It is too short. Life is too short."

You'll miss it if you're not looking carefully. If you're expecting nothing new, you won't see it. There, on the tree that stands taller than the rest, on the branch that is longer than the rest, is a funny kind of lump. It is narrow at the top and bigger at the bottom, attached to the underside of the branch. It was writhing and rippling but now it is still. Like a stream that has finally arrived at its destination. Inside the chrysalis there is a great dissolving. Caterpillar legs, organs, and muscles are melting down in an unstoppable act of destiny.

Chapter 11

It happened again. And again. I'd be at the yoga studio and right in the middle of wishing the experience would stop, all of a sudden it did. Not the class—my inner upheaval. It just went. Goodbye racing mind, goodbye self-consciousness, goodbye anything other than this moment. Up, down, side, side, my body was moving without my direction. I was a passenger being carried by breath. Forward, back, forward, back. Inhale. Exhale.

Pause.

Within the movement I entered into a deep stillness. It was a never-ending well of something I had never felt before. It was foreign and strange, as though it was something from outside me that was now in me. And I loved it. There was a part of me that relished fear, that adored anger and fueled jealousy. It was grasping and desperate, clingy and afraid. Controlling. It had been in charge for my entire life, and was growing stronger as I fed it by ignoring everything else. It had been licking its chops as I created a life based on filling that part of me up. But the never-ending well of that something inside me had quelled it. For a moment it had sat back on its haunches, confused by the feeling of relief when it was given permission to rest. The gaping hole was being filled up.

Around me, other people in the class were moving in unison: lunging, flowing, dancing, and sweating. I wanted to interrupt them and ask, "Do you feel this, too?" "Is this why you're here?" It didn't matter what their answer would be; I knew I wanted more. The skinny kid in my dream did, too. She was doing cartwheels.

I eat yoga for breakfast. I start reading books by all of the big-name teachers, inhaling everything they write about the how and why of the moving and breathing practice that can change a life. I read books with details of each and every single posture. Subscribe to yoga magazines. I watch video interviews and sit in workshops. The joy. The peace. The freedom. It had to have been there at one time, because it feels so deeply familiar—like the voice of a mother calling to her child through a crowd.

Had I ever been free of anxiety? Had I exited the womb and landed in the world curled tight in fear? My mom would tell me that as a baby I was smiling all the time. With my daffodil-blonde hair sticking out in all directions I'd smile, and smile, and smile. When I imagine that time, I see warm sunshine, soft blankets, and fuzzy caterpillars. Later, the willow tree tickling the earth and our foreheads as my sister and I slip through its branches to play beneath the canopy. Fresh green leaves turning to yellow and then dropping to the ground in the fall. Bare branches stark against a blue-gray sky as we lie on our backs on the toboggan, letting ourselves be pulled back up the hill.

When did the anxiety start? Being free from it makes me elated. Most classes, no matter what we're doing, I'm grinning. Ear-to-ear, cheek-splitting, wrinkling my face and leaving my muscles aching.

Chapter 12

Work is a place where I no longer fit in. When I think of my role in the world, I feel like a parasite.

But the red carpets, the VIP passes, the parties and grand openings! The deluxe trips and free spa treatments! What about those? There's a part of me that is convinced I've gone crazy. How can anyone leave all of this? I don't know. I truly don't. I just know that when I consider leaving it all I feel a great relief wash over me, and everything that feels tense and shackled lets go.

It was what I had wanted. But the part of me that wanted it was a part of myself that thought in terms of what was usually considered desirable, what was commonly held up as ideal or something to strive for. That part of me thought mostly in terms of external coordinates, orienting my actions and decisions toward things, ideas, and directions from outside me. Now I have gone inward, have looked through even the heart and into the soul—and seen the brilliance of what is possible when immersed in that place.

It is the great unknown. It is terrifying. It isn't what I have been taught or what anyone has ever recommended. But it is brilliant.

Sofie and I are coming back to the office after stopping by a just-opened clothing store to pick out our free pair of jeans. She's clapping her mitten-covered hands together, tugging her scarf up higher, and telling me how she's worried our listings editor, Jo, is dissatisfied, underutilized, and possibly bored.

"I'm worried she might leave," she says, looking across at me.

I stop, turn to look at her. "I need to tell you something."

Her face falls, her eyes get big, her forehead crinkles. "Are you leaving?"

I nod.

Sofie sighs, shrugs, "I guess, on the bright side, Jo will get promoted." She pauses, mulls it over. "What will you do?"

It's become common for me to look up to the sky when I'm feeling stuck or frustrated. I call out questions, sometimes demand answers, and then listen. At first, nothing happened. I'd lie there on the floor, or sit in my chair, and hear nothing but silence. But then I started listening wider. Not deeper. Wider. I realized that answers would come in different ways, and not always in that instant. I just had to pose the question. And then wait.

When I received the answer to how I'd get out of my job and into a new one, it came in the form of a dream. In this one, I met a woman with dark, curly hair and a great big laugh: she offered me a job working with her. A few weeks later, I met her in real life. Emily had started a new wellness consulting and coaching company. And she needed help. I had no idea what she did; I just liked that she understood why I wanted to leave.

"It's all about timing."

"So, what do you picture me doing?"

"We'll figure it out as we go along."

Edna writes a note on my goodbye card: "You're too good to stay out of this game." I look ahead, imagining freedom. Imagining less stress, more laughter. Peace.

The first four months of my new job are filled with writing copy for Emily's websites, crafting pamphlets, and sitting in meetings in coffee shops that meander and circle and never arrive anywhere definitive. Still, I am enthralled. Enthralled with meeting in coffee shops, with the sudden spontaneous trip Emily books for both of us to a small town up north, where we share a hotel room and she teaches a weekend of workshops. In the morning, I wake to her snores.

One day at a café, Emily sighs, looks out the window, and moans about the rain. The next day she is on the phone with me, letting me know she's going to Turkey for a month. "I need some time off. So, you should take time off, too." Three weeks later she is gone.

While Emily's gone I hear from her twice. The first is an e-mail about the men in Turkey and how she stands out from the other women. The second is to tell me she's ended her marriage.

When she gets back, Emily phones to tell me something she finds funny: "I just looked at our bank account. We can't afford to pay you anymore." She laughs, a short and bemused *isn't that so strange?* "ha" that comes out with a smile.

The pit in my stomach grows. And then it splits open. Like a balloon overfilled with air that pops with a shout, the gnawing sense of unease becomes freedom. I'd been let go. I was free. Free in a way I'd never been before. And might never be again.

Chapter 13

I'm doing it. I'm going to Paris. And Greece. I'll spend five days in the city of double kisses, cigarettes, croissants, and baguettes and then three weeks in Greece—which I don't know very much about, except that the picture of the retreat center I'll be staying at for a novel-writing immersion shows clear blue ocean, vast beaches, and stark white buildings.

I drag myself out of bed to the 7 a.m. yoga class. This is the class one of my favorite people attends. Monique. She's someone I wish everyone could meet, because everyone who does is inspired by her. She's seventy-five years old. Swims regularly. Does yoga nearly every day. Gets her hair and nails done, and can always be spotted with a pretty scarf around her neck. A retired French teacher, she and her husband Michael live half the year in Vancouver and the other half in Paris. She once said to me, "Every morning, even if I don't feel like it, I sing." Her current passion is learning Spanish, which she practices when she travels to Colombia—Colombia!

While she's there, she learns about the architecture, takes in the museums, and makes sure she's inside before the more treacherous hours of the night—you know, when the gangs come out. Monique and Michael rent out their apartment in Paris. I've got my fingers crossed.

When she hears what I've planned, Monique grabs my hand and starts a trot down the sidewalk. "Yes. Paris in the spring. We must see if it is free." Which, given her French accent, sounds like "We must zee eef eet eez frrree." Learning to imitate her accent has delighted me. I'm hoping it'll stand me in good stead when I'm in Paris. Maybe if I speak my minimal French with a perfect accent nobody will notice I have no idea what I'm saying.

Once she's pulled me down the sidewalk and up the stairs to her front porch, Monique flings open the door and calls out, "Michael, Lindsey is going to Paris." Seeing as I've never met Michael, it doesn't come as a surprise to me that the bespectacled man with soft gray hair looks confused at all the fuss when he peaks around the door into the hallway. He kisses me on the cheek anyway. I'm excited about getting used to that. Monique opens and closes drawers and rummages through papers before emerging again, scarf slipping off her shoulders, flourishing a calendar above her head. "Ici, we will see."

I'm holding my breath as she flips through the pages. She trails her finger down the weeks. And then: "You are in luck. It is free." She pencils in my name, tells me a price, and says, "Voila. You are booked."

I am booked.

Monique and Michael insist that I come back to go over the details of how to get from the airport to the apartment, and they want to tell me what they think I must see. How about today, I ask. But no, they're going to the new exhibit at the art gallery, they have a family lunch, and then Monique has Spanish lessons.

So I trail my way home after agreeing to come back next week.

The days are a roller coaster of elation and deep terror. "What are you doing? You're going to be mugged in Athens. You'll get lost in Paris." "I'll sit at cafes and eat chocolate croissants."

When it's finally time to see Michael and Monique again, I hop on my bike and head to their neighborhood. Cherry trees line the street, dotted with pink blossoms that float down, topsy-turvy, like fainting butterflies. Between the branches, the sun splashes golden paint on the asphalt. There's the smell of honeysuckle in the air, pungent and sweet. But I've forgotten where Michael and Monique live. I didn't write down the address. And I don't have their phone number. I ride up and down the street I think they live on, squinting at houses.

Inside, they tell me later, Michael is watching me go up and down, down and up their street. He calls out to Monique the first time I pass by, "Is that Lindsey?" And the second time, "Where is she going?" And the third, "There she goes again." The fact that I am utterly clueless about how to get to a place I was just at a week ago, in my own city and only a few blocks from the neighborhood I am most familiar with, might be part of the reason why Michael and Monique wouldn't give me the key until I'd come back for more directions.

They spend no less than two hours showing me photos and writing down instructions. Not of the sights they think I should see, but of the apartment and key landmarks on the route I'll take to get there. Monique has even drawn a shakily-lined map filled with delicious terms like *boulangerie*, *poissonnerie*, and *lingerie* shop. Michael explains: "It is because, if you are in the Metro and you are looking around, not knowing where you are going, it is not safe. You must be certain." He points. "There, that is where I'm going." They ask me to repeat back to them everything they tell me and convince me it's best if I come back again. So they can make sure I know everything I need to.

The following month I'm back for lunch at the dining room table, belly round from a four-course meal. Michael's books are stacked in corners, on tables, and the piano. The record player sits inside the bay window, and he's just lifted the needle from the Beethoven he had playing for us. The white lace curtains are drawn, leaving tiny poke-holes where the people passing by on the sidewalk appear in bits and pieces. They volley questions: When you get to the airport, what line do you take? From there you go where? Which direction do you walk when you get off the Metro and see the statue of the lion? What is the code for the apartment building? How do you hold the key? Finally, they decide I'm ready. Which is probably a good thing, given that my flight leaves in two days.

Chapter 14

Let's begin with this: I'm one of those people on the plane who at the end of the flight—no matter how short—is utterly spent. I need a four-hour nap after a one-hour flight. This is because I sincerely believe that I absolutely must only think positive, uplifting thoughts about the safety and rationale of hurtling 614 miles per hour through the sky, encased in 735,000 pounds of tin. If I'm not vigilant about my thoughts, if just one teeny tiny fear about free-falling 40,000 feet to the ocean below enters my head, that's it: we're all doomed. The plane will crash and I will die.

I have this power. I'm sure of it. The fact that every time I've flown I've had these kinds of thoughts and always landed safely? Irrelevant. And given the number of these kinds of thoughts that stream across my own personal CNN channel in my mind, accompanied by images of flaming wreckage and sobbing family members, it takes relentless awareness to stay on top of them. Plus a lock-down by nearly every muscle in my body, including my tongue.

This trip, I'm trying something new: talking to myself.

"There's nothing wrong with a plane moving side to side. That just happens, just like cars sometimes jiggle a little."

"Oh, OK—but now the plane is going up and down a little. The plane is going to crash and we're going to die!"

"Planes move up and down, too. Remember when Mike the pilot told me turbulence will never crash a plane?"

"Oh, OK—but wait, he also said that what actually crashes planes is human error. I bet there's a really tired pilot up there who's been flying long shifts and hasn't had enough coffee. I bet his eyelids are drooping right this second. And the plane is going to crash and we're going to die!"

At this point I give up on rationalizing and simply start telling myself to piss off. Over and over and over again. While attempting to maintain a conscious visualization of the airplane staying in the air until we land.

Fifteen minutes after setting foot on the second of two flights that will take me to Paris, I'm so jazzed on adrenaline that I'm rattling like I've had ten Red Bulls. And there's a sandy feeling in my mouth, which I think is small pieces of my molars. The person beside me has been itching to look out the window since the flight began, but as soon as I could I slammed that view of nothing but air out of my sight and stuck my ear buds in. Reading is out, since the movement of the pages as the plane jiggles just reminds me that I'm in an airplane that is riding on nothing but air. And so I choose my most soothing playlist and stick it on repeat, silently chanting along with Deva Premal. I have to go to the bathroom, but I'm certain that as soon as I lock the folding door behind me the plane will nosedive and I'll have no seatbelt on when it crumples into the Atlantic Ocean. So I'm holding it.

Tensing every muscle in my body, cramping my stomach, and avoiding all conversation that could potentially distract me from my thought vigilance definitely helps me remain calm. This is how I spend the entire flight. Chanting under my breath, and trying to breathe. Which looks like me every ten minutes or so realizing that I'm not, and gulping in an inhale big enough to fill Alaska and then exhaling it out my mouth with all the force I can muster. I also add a "Haaaaah" sound. I think I'm being pretty quiet about this, but I have my ear buds in so I'm not really sure. I have noticed that my seatmate has shifted as far to the other side of her seat as she can.

And then, finally, the craggy-voiced captain comes on the speakers to announce that we're beginning our descent. When the crew begins their walk down the aisles in preparation for landing, I hide my ear buds behind a scarf I've draped over my head like an old Austrian woman so they don't ask me to put them away. Finally we touch down, and with only a slight bounce. "We're on the ground!" I'm now manically smiling at everyone around me. My seatmate stares straight ahead.

Forty minutes later, I'm through customs and have hauled my suitcase—all sixty pounds of it—and my carry-on to the Metro line that will take me to the apartment. I join the crowd waiting on the platform, settling my suitcase beside a gentleman in his early 40s. Ten counts later—and although it sounds like an exaggeration it's not—my suitcase and I are nearly twenty feet away from him. As far as we can get, in fact. He seems to have interpreted my standing beside him as an invitation to press himself against me and stare at my chest, even though I've hardly got one.

The Metro arrives and I make a beeline for the very back. I try to pick a spot where I'm less visible, hunching down behind the seat in front of me. The man sits where he can stare, and when I move, he does, too. So, not so much a gentleman. For the rest of the ride, I attempt to fake nonchalance and focus on my guidebook.

Finally, it's my stop. I'm off the first Metro line and at the station Michael and Monique drilled into my head. I'm not used to riding underground; I feel like a mole, burrowing beneath the busy city and scurrying around in the dark. It takes ages for the train on the second Metro line to arrive at my stop. But finally I emerge. Into the city of light. And there is the lion, sitting proud on his perch. There are the cobblestone streets. There are the cafés that spill out onto the sidewalks, packed with people eating, smoking, and gesturing, even in mid-morning. There are the 19th-century buildings with their elaborate faces and chimneypots. There are the balconies that line the building faces looking out over the street. And there are the streets lined with bakeries, cheese and meat shops, and clothing boutiques that emanate effortless chic. Here is Paris. And here am I.

After dragging my suitcase through an airport, onto and off two Metro lines, up a flight of stairs, down a flight of stairs and up another flight of stairs, and then four blocks to the apartment, I'm beginning to think that maybe I didn't absolutely need to pack five sundresses. And six pairs of shoes. I'm tired, and my arms hurt. I'm standing at the entrance to the apartment courtyard, attempting to remember the code for the door. I'm also glaring at my suitcase; clearly it's to blame for my aching arms and despair at the thought of the four more flights of stairs ahead of me.

The door opens. Here is a Parisian with his young daughter, heading out for the day. She's about as tall as my waist, dressed in yellow, her brown hair styled in a bob. He has on brown loafers, brown corduroy pants, and a green button-up shirt. I attempt to lift my suitcase out of the way and over the doorframe into the courtyard. It doesn't budge. I try again. Nada. At the sight of me— hair falling in my face, sweat beading on my forehead, and dark circles under my eyes—and the reality that this slightly crazed-looking woman and her giant suitcase are blocking his only exit, he does something I soon learn is even more common in Paris than the leering. He says something in French and in such a kindly way that I feel safe in interpreting it as "May I help?"

In truth, I desperately want to say yes. I would love to have him carry my suitcase all the way to the top of those four flights of stairs with me following behind, panting elegantly. But even though I see his daughter and it's safe to assume he's a family man, I haven't yet let go of my first impression of French men.

So: "Oh, thank you, but no. I've got this."

He pauses, baffled. This woman so clearly hasn't "got this." I shake my head and he relents, throwing his hands up in the air as if to say, "She doesn't want help, ça va," and lifts his daughter over my suitcase, gingerly angling himself around it to follow after her.

You might think that someone's ascent of four simple flights of stairs would be uneventful. And if we were talking about any other someone I'd say you'd be right. But this is the girl who spent an hour locked behind a thankfully full-length bathroom stall door in a hostel washroom because she'd realized only after hearing the voices of all of the loudest, most-likely-to-never-forget-and-to-tease-mercilessly group of guys enter that she was in the men's. This is the girl who once folded nearly completely in half—head to toes—because she was marching so quickly toward the grocery store door that she didn't see the waist-height bar directly in front of her. The girl who once, driving home from university, ended up in a parade. (I felt so awkward about being there that I simply began waving in case it would convince people my parents' red Ford Taurus was part of it all.) I have a history of turning simple things into misadventures.

Let's just say that this simple thing-turned-misadventure involved multiple trips back down the stairs—to retrieve the dropped suitcase, which turned top over bottom, bottom over top so many times it could have won the gymnastics competition at the Olympics—and more bumps and thumps on my shins and ankles than an NHL hockey player.

But then I am there. In an apartment in Paris. The front door opens to a cozy one-bedroom with a galley kitchen, and a living room–dining room. The arched windows look out onto the famous rooftops and the street below. The leaves peeking in the windows are a green I immediately categorize as Paris green. It's a leaf color I haven't seen anywhere else—a soft sage that mixes the color of young buds with that of old vines. I look at it and think: *This is Paris. Fresh and new meets ancient and storied.*

And then I fall into bed and sleep.

Chapter 15

There are shutters on my windows. There are shutters on the windows of my apartment in Paris. And I am opening them out onto a street where a woman in a red coat is striding across the street, navy pants billowing, tan high heels clacking on the cobblestones, with her hair piled up into the perfectly messy bun. The one I can never pull off. Her scarf—of course, there is a scarf—is tucked at the nape of her neck. I can smell baking, the yeast and the flour, and the stink of exhaust. Right beneath me two men are arguing—in French. I am closing my eyes. I am breathing in. I am listening. Paris is waiting.

I bought a guide book but didn't really look at it until that moment on the bus—I wanted to wake up and say, "What do I want to do today?" and then wander out to see what I could find. There's no one in the courtyard, just a trailing vine with yellow blooms that fills the air with soft sweetness. It is quiet. Like the top of the inhale before a sentence begins to tumble out.

I open the door. Exhale. The people, the bakeries, the awnings above tables and chairs. The cigarette smoke.

"Sorry!" I yelp. A woman on a bike streams past, achingly fashionable, navigating lane changes in high heels, with a handbag.

I walk and walk. Drenching my senses. Avoiding bicycles. And cars. I have no plan, no goal for the day, no destination in mind. Everything is new and I am high on the joy of devouring it with my eyes. In Paris, there's a find around every corner. Cafés, boutiques, shops selling prints of the city from the eighteenth century. Museums. Bookshops. Cathedrals. I can see them all in front of me or beckoning around a corner. It is a feast.

Hours have passed. I am sated, but there's somewhere I need to go. It's not that famous cathedrals are high on my list. It's people, not buildings, that light me up. But there's an invitation, a wordless call. And a curiosity about what it will lead to.

At Notre-Dame there's a crush of people waiting to get in, most with cameras hanging around their necks. The line snakes down the stairs and into the square. As I stand waiting, what at first seems like a cacophony of contrasting languages gradually emerges as a harmony of human voices. Gothic towers looming high above us, the cathedral watches. There are eyes everywhere: those of kings from the Old Testament, and of gargoyles looking out from beneath hooded lids. The rose windows emanate the heart of the structure outward. It's the windows that are calling. They are a kaleidoscope of color, a rainbow of restrained proportions, but luminescent nonetheless.

Once inside, sunlight spins through tinted glass, touches down on stone arches and walls, makes its way to the wooden pews where I sit, growing ever more calm, ever more light. I haven't prayed much. But I find my head bowing, eyes closing as the colors ebb and flow together. And then I feel it: that same sense of all-encompassing peace. My entire body senses it. I soften. I breathe. There is a hum vibrating in the air around me. It's a bit like the buzz of bumblebees and makes me feel like I'm outside on a spring day, lying in the grass beneath a tree. The hum and I sit quietly together for I don't know how long, just sharing some serenity in the city of light.

Ping! Ping. Ping. Something is tapping on the edge of my consciousness, steadfastly pulling me up out of sleep. What is that sound? I wake up and realize that Paris is experiencing a typical torrential downpour, and it seems the roof of the apartment has given up. Water is raking through the seam where the wall meets the ceiling. I lay out every single pot and then wake up twice more that night to empty them. I spend the next two days close to the apartment so I can keep an eye on the rain that's collecting in all the vessels I can find. Everything is sopping wet.

And then, sun. I'm walking past the Louvre when the clouds part. I've just spotted a cute guy with a red bike standing beside a bike-tour sign. I take the sun as a sign, too, and inch over to ask him what the tour is about. I've actually begun to do what I imagined: speak English with a French accent—completely unintentionally. So he looks at me, baffled. And then begins speaking English. With a perfect French accent. He's grinning. I'm grinning. And then I'm walking with him into a dark underground parking lot, and for a moment I wonder what the hell I'm doing. But then I see the eight other people milling around a rack of identical red bikes.

Ten minutes later, I'm riding a bike through Paris. I'm biking through Paris! "Don't worry when the locals honk at you," our guide tells us. "That's just their way of saying 'Welcome to Paris.'" We stream past the Louvre, a high school where the cigarette smoke in the air signals the mid-morning break, the apartment Victor Hugo lived in, and artwork by English artist and activist Banksy, tucked high on the corners of ornate buildings. When it's time to stop for lunch, our guide helps us order in French. My verb tenses are wrong, but my accent is still good. We sit at tiny round tables on the sidewalk and eat our baguette sandwiches. Just like the locals.

At the end of the tour we drop off our bikes and I wander back to the area around the Louvre. I've just spent the day riding around Paris on a bicycle. With a cute French guide. And now I'm finding my way to the Champs-Élysées. Without a guide. I've been finding my way. In fact, I've gotten everywhere I want to go without getting lost. I'm the girl who once received a compass for her car from her brother-in-law for Christmas. I had turned left instead of right after visiting my sister at their apartment, and drove an hour in the wrong direction, only to lock my keys in the car after finally pulling into a gas station to buy a map. He and my sister had driven out with the spare set of keys. I'm that girl.

Then again, maybe I'm not.

I'm getting strong. I'm getting confident. And I'm getting on a bus that will take me where I want to go.

The bus is packed. It's rush hour. A round-bellied man with a shiny nose is staring at me. I guess it's just more of a thing here. But now I don't feel as threatened or scared. They do seem to look a lot and for a lot longer than I'd like, but that's all they seem to do. So when it's time to get off I strut toward him with my head held high, looking him square in the eye. *You? You don't scare me.* I'm even managing to stay that confident as I squeeze past him, my chest being squished by his shoulder. In the moment when I get stuck beside him, waiting for the person in front of me to exit, he turns to me and says, "*Voulez-vous couchez avec moi?*"

Luckily for me, a gaggle of female pop stars has just released a collaborative hit that includes this line, which we've all learned means "Will you sleep with me?" I have a momentary upswing of celebratory thought along the line of, "Hey, I understood what he said," before I realize that he said *that.* I scramble through the crush of people and speed-walk down the sidewalk, turning every five steps or so to look behind me.

It delights me that at the Champs-Élysées there's a lineup at Louis Vuitton, and a security guard stands at the entrance in a pinstripe gray suit and charcoal tie. He steps aside as three women in black burkas trimmed with gold float out to their waiting limo, their head scarves catching in the wind.

In the Latin Quarter, there are postcards of nude men and women in among the reprints of nature scenes by Manet and Monet. At the Jardin du Luxembourg, I eat lunch by a pond dotted with sailboats being guided by small boys chewing their lips in concentration. At Les Deux Magots—a favorite café of Hemingway's—the patio is full, but inside there are only a few tables taken, by Japanese tourists. I see a stunning, tall, thin girl in leather pants and a giant distressed sweatshirt stalking down a sidewalk in the Place Vendôme. She has perfectly messy hair under a baseball cap with *VOGUE* across the front in gold metal lettering, and I just *know* that she's a model.

Days pass this way, in a blur of iconic sights, timeless moments, and . . . pastries. I can't stop eating pastries. I've started doing the French woman thing where you order a few and only eat a few bites. (I added the "order a few" part.)

Chapter 16

The morning of my flight to Athens it isn't raining and I've packed my enormous suitcase again. It won't fit through the turnstile at the Metro station. I was late leaving the apartment, and I know for sure the time I allowed for myself to get to the airport before boarding didn't accommodate being late. I immediately start to worry I'm going to miss my flight. I attempt to lift my suitcase up and over the turnstile. No go. I try to shove it through. No go. I feel a tap on my shoulder, and a very nicely dressed Frenchman points to swinging double doors. Ah. I slide through and a few minutes later I'm on the train headed to the airport.

I'm thinking about Athens—the Parthenon, the Acropolis, the streets lined with vendors—when I hear the name of the next station being announced. Shit. I've missed my stop. I thought I was on a line that would take me straight to the airport. It looks like I should have gotten off and switched three stops back. I lunge for my suitcase and haul it onto the platform. I'm in a small French town with red-roofed brick houses, a horse standing in a field, and one main street. I check my watch. I have thirty minutes before my flight is due to leave. I need a taxi.

My suitcase and the backs of my ankles have become great friends. They never want to part. This becomes painfully obvious when I have to drag it up a flight of stairs and down a flight of stairs to cross over to where I can exit the platform. I launch myself through the double doors, only to see the message "Erreur Erreur" flash before me. I didn't validate my ticket before getting on the train. I can't get through the double doors in front of me, and I also can't back out of the double doors behind me. It seems the French transit police have learned a lot from live animal traps. I'm pushing forward, pushing backward, and just like a deer caught in a trap, I'm stuck and starting to panic. There doesn't seem to be anyone around who can help. Just nicely dressed men and women on their way to work. No uniformed transit people. Nobody. Until a hand appears over the double doors behind me, emerging from a suit sleeve to flash a transit pass over the reader so the doors in front will open. I'm free. "Merci," I shout as the man retreats and leaps onto his train.

There's a taxi stand across the street. I race toward it and plant myself beside the bench. It's an eternal ten minutes before I realize that I'm not in Kansas anymore. This isn't a city and the taxis don't come every five minutes or so. There's probably only one or two in this entire town. And I don't have a phone to call one. So I'm going to have to catch the train back, change trains, and get on the one that will take me to the shuttle to the airport, where I'll need to check in, drop my suitcase, and go through security. All in under twenty minutes. I race for the train platform again. Down a flight of stairs, cross over, up a flight of stairs, down a flight of stairs.

I know for many people the idea of a missed flight isn't cause for anxiety. For many people, a missed flight is a no-big-deal-I'll-just-catch-the-next-one kind of shrug of the shoulders. They take it in stride, rearrange their schedule, call whoever they need to call, and then order a glass of wine. I'm not one of those people. My default mode when something doesn't go according to plan like this is to, well, basically freak right out.

Which I begin to do with great efficacy right there on the station platform. I've even started to do my airplane breathing. Enormous inhale, huge exhale, "Haaaah." It's all very normal. I check my watch. There's now only fifteen minutes before my flight is due to leave. I'm in full-on panic mode, heart pounding, mind racing, vision narrowed. Everything's fuzzy. For the second time on this trip, I pray. Only this time, I'm not just sitting quietly feeling like springtime in an iconic church. I've got my hands pressed together high above my head, and I'm still doing my airplane breathing. In between breaths, I'm silently asking God for help. "Please help me. I don't want to have a panic attack right here. I don't want to miss my flight." I open my eyes hoping for a miracle. Hoping for the train to arrive right that second. Nada.

Just like in the movies, I hear nothing but crickets.

But something strange has happened. My watch seems to have stopped. It has been more than two minutes since I last checked it, back at the taxi stand. *Oh, wonderful, on top of it all.* The train finally pulls up. It's about a foot and a half up to the train car from the platform. I'm looking at it helplessly when a small blonde woman looks down at me with a little smile and asks, "Do you need help?" Oh, yes please. "Oui, merci." I'm about to grasp the handle when she does it herself, and lifts my giant suitcase onto the train. With one hand. The doors close behind me. She asks if I'm OK, and then disappears.

When the doors open at the next station there's no one waiting to get on the train. It's eerily quiet. Across the platform there's a spotty hedge that looks like it's not getting enough water. But there's a song playing through the speakers usually reserved only for announcements. I've never heard music being played through the speakers at a Metro station in Paris. I've never heard music being played through speakers at a Metro station in any city. And yet here is a tune floating out over the empty platform and onto the train. It goes, "Don't worry, be happy."

I know.

I've begun to calm down. I get off the train, change to another one, and hop on the shuttle to the terminal. I'm running to the check-in and luggage drop-off desk. They smile and take my bags. I'm running to the moving walkway that will take me to my gate. It's jammed with a crush of people that I wiggle myself in beside for the ride. I've stopped checking my watch because each time I do—despite all the running I'm doing—it's obviously running slow. There's no way I've done all of this in under ten minutes.

I run down the hall and around the corner, and come to a near-screeching halt at the gate I was meant to be at thirty minutes ago. The attendant at the counter smiles and checks my passport, confirms I'm getting on the right flight, and waves me on my way.

I board the plane and find my seat. Fasten my seatbelt. Check my watch. It reads the exact time our flight was scheduled to leave. Somehow I managed to wait for a taxi, give up on waiting for a taxi, wait for a train, board a train, ride it three stops, get off, wait for another train, get on that train, ride to the airport shuttle, get on the shuttle, check my bags and check in for my flight, go through security, get to my gate, and board my flight—all in under thirty minutes. I'm baffled.

But then I realize that I felt taken care of and watched over the entire time I was in Paris. Each time I felt the surge of mild panic, somebody would arrive to offer help. The man at the apartment when I first got there, the man who directed me through the first set of double doors at the station that morning, the man who freed me from the ones I was stuck in at the next station, the woman who lifted my suitcase. The song on the speakers at the train station. There was always someone, or something, there to reassure me.

This calms me enough that I—me!—actually manage to fall asleep on the flight to Athens.

I've been daydreaming of white limestone buildings, blue skies, and endlessly clear ocean.

The hotel I've booked in Athens was recommended to me by the brother of a friend of mine—a guy who likes to backpack in unusual places and stay at spots where he can get the most bang for his buck. Although the top-floor lounge has a rooftop view of the Acropolis, my room is just a bit larger than my single bed. So my suitcase takes up most of the remaining space. And the shower is just a few inches wider than my shoulders. A few days ago, my friend forwarded me an e-mail from her brother, in which he wrote, "I didn't realize when you were asking for recommendations on places to stay in Athens it was for your friend Lindsey. The area I suggested is not the safest. She'll need to be very careful if she goes out at night."

I'm sure spending my evenings on the roof with a crew of visiting American university students all angling for the same patchy Wi-Fi as I am counts as lapping up the local sights. At least from the lounge we have a 180-degree view. From this vantage point, Athens looks like it was extended a few blocks at a time by a planner who kept changing his mind. Spider-web streets stretch out at haphazard angles, lined with buildings that each shout out their own unique blueprint, billboards with ads for sausage and pop, and telephone lines. There are stray dogs wherever you find the most people.

High on the hilltop sits the Acropolis. The Parthenon, the Propylaia, the Erechtheion, and the temple of Athena Nike all look down on the busyness of the roads unfurling and edging their way out to the city's perimeter. The Korai stand holding the weight of the sky on their shoulders. Wandering around the Acropolis and surrounding neighborhood shops the next day, I'm caught between lust for the fabrics, sandals, and dried figs, and an unshakeable sense that the soul of this ancient storied city has been lost.

Three nights later, my perception of Athens has further entrenched itself. Weariness sets in as I lie down to sleep in a new hotel—the one my retreat center group is scheduled to leave from in the morning. This one has an open-air courtyard with chaise lounges and tables and chairs dotting the corners and a fountain in the middle. There are giant potted palm trees in the lobby and the guest reception desk stretches over six metres. As I wandered around before bed I spotted a few people who looked like they'd just met but had something in common, all travelers who were having the gently stilted, curious-about-each-other kind of conversation you have with someone about whom you're figuring out how much more you want to see.

There are three pillows and a fluffy white duvet on my single bed, palm fronds in the wallpaper, and a view of the courtyard out the window in the shared room I've signed up for—but no sign of my roommate for the night. Tucked under the covers, I'm lost in tapping away at my laptop, reliving Paris, when I realize it's midnight and my roommate for the night still hasn't arrived. It's odd to be going to bed not knowing who I'll wake up with.

I am dreaming of a daffodil. She is bright like the face of a child about to get an ice-cream cone. And just as clear. She has no roots; she floats. There is a breeze that dances her between the clouds. She is being carried. It is beautiful. The daffodil is lifted higher, higher. There is a thud, a scraping sound, a word thrown out like a spear, a presence in the room. The daffodil bursts and so does the dream.

Squinting in the sudden brightness of the overhead light, my heart hammering, I can make out a woman with fuzzy brown hair, a long purple skirt, and a purse that's falling from her shoulder as she struggles to drag her suitcase into a corner. She is looking at the bed the way a woman on a diet looks at cupcakes. She is giving up on tucking her suitcase out of the way, dropping her purse to the floor, and falling face-first onto the duvet, arms and legs like a starfish. She moans.

I was once sitting beside a small boy, a three-year-old, reading him a bedtime story. He was entranced—so caught up in the turtle and the rabbit that his constant movement was stilled. Until—he wasn't. One moment he was big-eyed and leaning forward and the next he exhaled, turned his head to one side, and was gone into sleep. I couldn't believe it. I whispered his name, peered into his face, touched his chest to see if he had stopped breathing. His chest rose and fell with the deep and steady rhythm of sleep.

This woman falls asleep like that. I hate her a little.

Morning is not welcome. The shrilling of my alarm gets my fury too—I pound it off with my fist. The clock reads 8 a.m.

"I'm late!"

"Oh yes," my roommate nods from beneath the covers, British accent piquing my ears when she says, "It's been going off for over an hour now."

I'm late. The covers are off. My clothes are on the floor. The bathroom light is still on and in the mirror

I see dark circles and enormous hair. My foot is stuck in my pants, my toothpaste tube falls onto the floor, the concealer rolls after it. I bump my hip against the counter's edge while hopping on one foot. Shit.

My foot finds its way through my pantleg. Two feet on the floor. The concealer is tucked back into my case. Toothpaste makes it onto my toothbrush. I rub my hip while brushing my teeth. Zip. I have to sit on my suitcase. But it closes, sandals slip on my feet, and the door to the room ejects me with a resounding click.

I pluck two hard-boiled eggs from the buffet and pour some orange juice before stepping up to the group that is milling around a tall, balding, nattily dressed man with glasses and a clipboard.

"I'm Allan," he says as he nods at me, ticking my name off the list. The silver cross at his neck shifts beneath his shirt collar.

Around me are all the people who've signed up for two weeks at the Eirene Retreat Center, on a small island in the Cyclades, an archipelago in the Aegean Sea. There's a slender blonde woman with a matching skirt and blouse, her hair coiled up in a smooth bun; a mop-haired guy in board shorts and a button-up dress shirt, towering over us; and a tall, broad-shouldered, silver-haired woman with red bangles, red reading glasses on a silver chain, and multiple oversize rings. There are others, each in their own way adding some color, all flapping and pecking in a way that suggests a flock of parrots—half a tour-bus-full, in fact—and as I follow them to board the bus that will take us to the ferry terminal, they blend together in a sea of faces and excited voices.

The bus heaves into gear and lumbers onto the highway that will take us out of Athens. As the buildings grow farther apart and the rolling hills dotted with olive trees, juniper, and oleander shrubs rise and ebb away out the window, the voices grow quiet. We're all immersed in watching the unfolding landscape. We also know this: at the end of our six-hour trek, we'll have wound our way through small valley towns and down hillsides steeped in history, to the edge of the Aegean Sea. From there, we'll board a ferry that will take us to an island in the midst of that sea, and it's there that what we've all been dreaming of will take flight.

The island that we'll call home for the next two weeks lingers at the edge of our minds, tantalizing us with visions of white limestone buildings facing the sea, a town square ringed with balconies and a bakery, clothing store, and pharmacy, and a long earthen staircase winding its way down a cliff to the sand and waves below. We catch glimpses of the open sea as we make our way between towns and up and over hills. Flashes of sunlight glint off the clear blue.

Soon the hillsides and glimpses of blue are crowded out by narrow streets and tightly packed buildings. Dark-haired men and women with sun-browned skin press themselves against the walls as our bus inches down streets that were built for carriages and donkeys. We look down to find that they are looking back up at us, either inquisitively or scowling ear to ear.

A rooster crows. A woman flaps a tea towel from her upstairs window. Our driver curses, pressing the brakes hard, as a young boy chases a ball into the street.

The nose of the bus pulls out from the crush of buildings and there is the open sea, wide and clear as glass, still enough that as we trip down the stairs and onto the dock where we'll board our ferry we can see down to where silvery fish are darting in the shadows, above the sand.

The Aegean Sea.

Chapter 17

Legend has it that King Age leapt to his death into this sea because his son sailed home on black sails instead of white. King Age thought he was dead. I imagine an ocean floor filled with relics—chests, sunken ships, bounty meant for other cities, and bones.

Our ferry is dusted with dirt and, inside, filled with cigarette smoke. It rocks slightly from side to side as we pull away from the dock. We're scattered around the benches on the upper deck, watching the land behind us get smaller and the silhouette in front become a firm outline of an island.

"Are you working on a novel?"

There's a small-boned girl with giant sunglasses and scuffed shoes sitting beside me. She reminds me of a wren with her dark hair and darting eyes. She starts and stops her movements before she's finished them. She opens her mouth to speak and then closes it again, stands up halfway and then sits down, midway through moving one arm to her side decides it's better resting on her lap. She's been taking her sunglasses off and putting them on again, squinting into the sun each time it bathes her naked face.

I shake my head.

"No. I'm here because I need . . ." I trail off. I don't know what to say. The reason I chose to travel across the world to spend two weeks at a novel-writing retreat had nothing to do with having a novel to write. It had everything to do with having a part of me that was dying come back to life. I turn to look at the wren-girl, her blinking eyes turned up at me, head tipped over to one side. I imagine the words tumbling out of my mouth, the whole story from start to finish: *I dismantled my life. It didn't fit me anymore.*

Instead, I say, "I just want to see what happens."

She nods. Puts her sunglasses on. Looks back out at the waves.

The island, and our port, is coming closer. Tucked into the foot of the hills is an inlet ringed with small homes and a shack with a sign that reads "Fresh fish." At least I think it does, given that it looks like almost every other fish shack, but I can't be sure because I didn't hone any Greek-speaking or -reading skills before I arrived. Fishing boats painted red, blue, and yellow bob in the water. Rising up from the port are white stone buildings tucked into the hillside. Waving at us from the dock is a man with rosy red cheeks like Santa Claus, but with a face more impish than jovial. He grips Allan in a tight hug as we gather around, stretching arms and legs and watching for our luggage.

Strange. It smells like home. It smells like my grandparents' land, like the trees in the woods behind their house, like the scent carried on the breeze that would come down the mountains in the evening as the sun went down. So. Not strange. Strangely familiar.

Cobblestone streets weave among the white houses, apartments, and shops dotted with cascading flowers, pink and fragrant in the heat of the sun. Our luggage is carted one piece at a time to a flatbed truck with two-by-four sides and stacked into a lazy precarious pile by a heaving, grumbling man with a round nose and belly. He'll take our luggage on his truck as far as he can, we're told, but the streets are too steep and too narrow for him to bring it all the way to the doors of the apartments we're staying in. We'll find it in a pile at the top of the hill just over there, through the stores and past the town square, just beyond the only hotel in town, where we'll pick it up and bring it the rest of the way.

It'll be waiting for us when we arrive.

We look at each other with eyes gone big and round, eyebrows lifted.

The wren-girl darts toward her suitcase and then stops as it's hauled onto the pile, her luggage tag with "Nancy" spelled out carefully above her home address flapping helplessly on its side.

"I just wanted to check it first," she says, hands winding through the ends of her hair.

We're a scattered, straggling crew in the street leading to the retreat center, with Allan striding in front, pointing out landmarks: the bakery where we need to remember to turn right, the hostel where we duck left, the drugstore where we can buy emergency supplies—Band-Aids, things like Advil and Tylenol, and five-hundred-Euro sunglasses. He calls back at us repeatedly to keep up the pace, but we can't stop slowing to stare at the view. The higher we climb, the more the ocean behind us sparkles, the deeper the blue gets, and the larger the sky grows. At the end of the line is Harvey, the red-cheeked man who was waving from the dock, introduced to us as we filed off the ferry as the Eirene Retreat Center's Life Learnings program director. Harvey is huggable, like a great round teddy bear whose girth nearly matches his height. He's out of breath and pausing to catch it every few feet or so, looking happily up at us filing in front of him, beaming as though we've already learned something, just by being here.

We climb and wind through the narrow streets until there on the left is a pile of luggage. We rush it, doves turned into grasping crows, each of us half-laughing with relief at the sight of it there, just where they said it would be. Allan stands in the center of us all, more than a foot taller than everyone, including me, and hands out keys while pointing out directions. We're to drag our suitcases down the streets to the apartments we've been assigned to, drop them off, and then head straight back up the hill to the center for our official welcome and then dinner. He pauses, one corner of his mouth turned up and the corners of his eyes crinkled as he considers me and my giant suitcase. He opens his mouth, words beginning, and then closes it again. Instead, he just grins, shakes his head, and turns to walk up the rest of the hill.

Suitcase at my heels, I'm nearly there when I pass a patio with a small round wrought-iron table and single chair out front. There's a blue scarf dropped on the seat of the chair and a glass of water with ice and a slice of lemon, dripping condensation onto the tabletop. A notebook lies open beside it, pages rising, lifting, and then turning over in the breeze. I catch my breath. The door to the apartment is open, and someone is moving inside. Bent over a dresser, a woman in a black sundress and daisy flip-flops is sifting through the contents of a drawer, speaking softly. Her hair is pulled up in a haphazard bun and brown-black pieces spring lazily from the elastic, framing her face. The owner of the scarf. And the notebook. She's looking for something. She turns and looks up, and before she can catch me watching I pull away.

Two doors down is apartment number seven. The key turns in the lock and the door swings wide. Inside is a single bed draped in a brown, red, and blue comforter; a wooden dresser; and a small table with two chairs. There's a galley kitchen with a small fridge, stove, and sink. There's no division between the shower and the rest of the bathroom, and the toilet sits just beside the handheld showerhead, which hooks onto the wall at about knee height. I'll need to learn how to wash my hair one-handed. Either that, or shower lying on the floor.

It's the stairs that attract me the most. I can tell there's sunlight up there. Up a flight of stairs with a small landing I find another bed, this one a double, and French doors that open out onto my very own rooftop patio. From here I can see the ocean, the rooftops of the village trundling down the hillside, and the Eirene Retreat Center up at the top. Tucked into the hill, it has an enormous patio framed with fig and pomegranate trees. The patio is lined with long tables and benches, and just above it is a nook of a room, all windows and wood frames, too small to be for a group, too oddly placed to be for sleeping. The rest of the center is a building two floors high, with blue-shuttered windows above and clay walls etched with suns, moons, and stars below.

It's on the patio that we first gather, benches scraping and apologies murmured as we bump into each other while shuffling into place. The woman in the black sundress has her scarf on now and sunglasses on top of her head. She sits at a table with Allan, Harvey, and two other women, both wearing linen shifts and Birkenstocks. A small woman in a red slip dress with defined biceps and calves holds a clipboard and is calling for our attention. She smiles, pausing to meet eyes with each person.

"Welcome to the Eirene Retreat Center."

"The center was founded thirty years ago as a space for people to come for relief, to rest from the busyness of the world and connect with other people like them."

The tall mop-haired guy in the board shorts and button-up leans across the table, speaking through the corner of his mouth: "I'm just here for the food."

The woman in the red slip dress frowns a little, pausing in her recitation, then continues, "For thirty years, people from all over the world—"

"But mostly Brits," quips the mop. Red slip dress narrows her eyes.

"—from all over the world have come here and returned home feeling transformed. Many of our guests come back year after year, bringing friends and family. Our faculty has included renowned teachers, each experts in their chosen profession. Harvey, our Life Learnings program director, has been with us for over a decade."

Mop-hair can't let up: "Guess he likes the food, too," he whispers across the table.

Red slip dress sighs, lowers her clipboard, and walks over to stand in front of him.

"Please tell me your name."

Shrinking a little into his chair, mop-hair looks up, chagrined.

"It's Michael."

"Michael, I'm Elana. I'm the assistant manager at Eirene and one of the things I love about my job is welcoming our new participants. You are making that very difficult."

Michael's resigned "Sorry" comes out with the kind of sigh heard from kids used to being told to quiet down. Elana nods, and then walks back to the table where Allan, Harvey, the woman in the black sundress, and the two other women in linen are sitting. "These wonderful people" she says, gesturing toward them, "are your faculty and managing director. They'll each take a few minutes to tell you a little about themselves."

Harvey stands, and the Life Learnings participants lean in. He talks about how much he loves what he does, how important this time will be, and how great the food is. The two women in linen are next. The older one, with dark gray hair and wire-rimmed glasses, speaks for both of them, the younger one with long red hair and pale, freckled skin nodding along happily. When she's finished,

I think I've just witnessed someone kind and earnest talking in a very impassioned way about something vaguely like Reiki but also like theatre improv, and I have no idea what it all means. It seems that no one else does either. Nobody has signed up for the Reiki improv program, and Allan tells us that part of our program tomorrow morning will involve a short introductory workshop on what the linen ladies are up to. We nod.

The woman in the black sundress is next. It's hard to tell for sure, even though I've been watching her since we arrived, but she seems to be attempting to keep a smiley kind of smirk from her face. A few times I've seen her fake a cough, covering her mouth with her hand while her eyes keep laughing. She stands and pauses to look around at the faces trained her way.

"Who among you is in the writing program?"

Hands are raised around the patio. Mine. Nancy's. The older woman with silver hair and broad shoulders. A messy-haired small man with large glasses and a pocket protector. A red-haired woman in a navy dress with bags under her eyes and a French braid. Michael waves his hand back and forth, and then up and down.

"I'm Katherine."

Katherine moves out from behind the table and walks to the middle of the space. She raises both her hands and takes a slow spin. We follow her eyes, taking in the rooftop, the fig and pomegranate trees, the cloudless sky and then finally, right behind us, the ocean. "All of this," she says, letting her hands fall to her sides, "is for all of you. Every leaf, every sunbeam, every breeze that carries the scent of sycamore trees. It's all for all of us. Writers get to claim it, make it their own, shape a world within this world, create something that is of all of this but not in it. Over these next weeks, I'm going to challenge you. I'm going to challenge you to rise out of your everyday reality, to see things as you've never seen them before, to look through the eyes and record through the lens of someone who is not just an observer. Someone who is a writer."

Now I know why I've been captivated. I don't just *like* her. I want to *be* her. I watch her return to her seat. We're clapping. We can't help it. "She's great," murmurs Nancy. Even Michael is awed; he's become entirely serious.

Elana is speaking, telling us that dinner will be served on the patio shortly, and breakfast will be served promptly at eight-thirty tomorrow. The morning yoga session begins at seven.

Michael is leaning over again, glancing left and then right before leaning his chin on his hand and starting to speak, his tone hushed and conspiratorial.

"She missed something," he says. Nancy and I lean forward. "Back when it started, the center used to do a kind of therapy." We lean closer. "Primal scream therapy." We look at each other and then back at Michael. "The locals used to hear it from the street." Across the patio, dinner has arrived and Harvey is filling his plate and talking with Katherine.

Later that evening, I walk down the cobblestone streets and through the warren of buildings. The air is still warm, but as the sun sets the breeze carries a coolness that speaks of ocean water, gulls, and lapping waves on dark, damp sand. Passing by Katherine's apartment, I see her at the small table beneath the window, a lamp lighting the notebook she's writing in. I see her pause and look up to stare absently just in front of her, one corner of her mouth lifted in a smile. I wonder what she's writing, and if we'll ever get to read it.

The key turns in the lock and the door slides open. Inside it is dark, even with the two table lamps switched on. In the dim light it's easy to start to feel tired, and after a shower, even though I climb into bed with the full intention of recording it all in my journal, I can't keep my eyes open. Sleep cocoons me like a comforter, and in a way I've never really known. I'm astonished to find myself woken up by my alarm clock, having slept through the night.

The morning sun has risen high by seven in the morning and I'm hopping from one foot to the other on the rooftop patio as I lay out my yoga mat—the floor burns beneath my feet. There's a bird call that I don't recognize but that lilts and falls in a way that makes me think of the robins I'd pause to listen to as a child, standing at my window watching the world wake up. In fact, there's much about this place that reminds me of places I loved as a kid, and instead of moving through my usual morning yoga routine, I end up sitting on the mat and remembering.

The circle of young trees I'd tuck myself away in to read. The roof of my grandpa's garage that I'd climb up to, even though I wasn't allowed, to lie flat on my back and stare at the clouds. The creek that passed through the forest we'd explore as a family, curling into a pool beneath rocks with moss that created curtains hiding miniature caves. Our backyard, where in the summer I lay for hours in the sun, watching the beetles and worms work their way over and through the dirt in the garden. One step back toward that girl I'd forgotten and suddenly I'm in her world again, dreaming.

The walk to Eirene is cushioned by these remembrances, and I'm feeling light when I come up behind Nancy. She's crying.

"Are you OK?"

She looks up at me beneath eyelashes thickened with tears and I keenly feel the lightness vanish and the uneven stones beneath my feet.

"I'm sorry. I'm so emotional now. Since the fall."

"As in the season, you mean?"

"No, a few months ago I slipped while I was ice skating. I don't remember much. I woke up in the hospital."

"God. That sounds scary."

"It was. And, you know, since then I can't remember things as well. And I cry even more easily than before. And I was already a crier." Nancy smiles and lets slip a small rueful laugh.

I'm not sure if this small, bird–like girl will break if I wrap her in a hug, so instead I gently pat her on the arm.

"I cry easily, too." We walk along in silence for a while, and then, as we near the entrance to the retreat center, I ask, "What was making you sad?"

Nancy turns to me and her shoulders droop. "My boyfriend asked me to marry him."

Chapter 18

Laid out on a table are platters of toast, fresh fruit salad, yogurt with honey, hard-boiled eggs, and porridge with nuts, raisins, brown sugar, and cream. Tea, coffee, and orange juice is on a side table in the sitting room off the patio. Only three of us scoop up the goopy, mushy oats: me, Michael, and the silver-haired woman—she's still wearing her red bangles, red reading glasses on a silver chain, and multiple oversize rings.

"My husband loathes this stuff," she says. "It's one thing I love about traveling without him; I get to be free of his complaints about the food."

"He doesn't like what you like?"

"He thinks porridge should be fed only to farm animals. I tell him he's too patrician for his lineage. The man grew up on a farm." We're sitting down across from each other at one of the long and narrow tables when she tips her head to one side and slides her glasses onto her nose: "I'm Margaret."

Margaret then launches into a litany of questions, asking one after the other until I feel spent, having shared nearly all of the surface details of my biography. Finally, she lands on the one I've been dreading: "What's your novel about?"

Faced with the choice between the honest explanation, delving deeper and painfully, and keeping a buffer between my unsettled places and Margaret's piercing eyes, I find myself reverting to a version of the same answer I gave Nancy: "I just want to see what I can do." It's not the truth, but the truth isn't linear, or logical, or rational. In response, Margaret simply raises her eyebrows, and then returns to her porridge.

All around us are the murmurs and contented, filled-up sighs of our new and temporary community. We sit with the sun warming our backs, the ocean beyond, and the rustle of the leaves of the fig tree, getting comfortable with each other—and already starting to notice subtle character traits in the people who yesterday seemed a mass of strangeness. Especially, it would seem, the writers among us. It's comforting to note that the others in my group also seem to be slightly more watchful than the rest, a certain alertness and keen listening that marks them as people used to observing.

The observing looks like reticence to Karan, the facilitator of the Reiki-improv intro session the entire tribe attends after breakfast. She keeps calling us by name, encouraging us to more fully express the energy of a young owl ducking under a rock, a warrior princess stalking through the jungle, or a toddler with dirty nappies. "It's my friends who'll have dirty nappies from laughing so hard when I tell them how I started my writing retreat," quips Michael as we waddle past each other. When the writing group gathers on a small patio tucked beneath an olive tree that shields us from the road, we can't help but laugh when Michael does his version of the warrior princess.

Katherine has spent the morning with the other facilitators and Elana and Allan. Today, her hair is down around her face, and her sunglasses lie on the table. Stacked in front of her are a single-page outline of our program and four books: three of her novels and her book on how to write one.

We look at her, waiting. She is looking around the table, eyes moving from one face to the next, as she asks for our names and checks them off her list. "This will be the last time I take attendance," she tells us, putting the paper to the side. "Your participation in this program is up to you." Picking up the novel at the top of the stack, she opens it to a page already marked by a blue bookmark and begins to read:

"Shading her eyes from the sun, Anna could make out the shape of a man moving toward her across the sand. He wasn't hurrying, wasn't rushing, wasn't moving quickly. It was the steady, methodical and direct line he was making toward her that made her heart quicken. It was the way his gaze never wavered from the spot she lay, and the set of his jaw." Katherine puts the book down and looks at our group: "What do we know about the man approaching Anna?"

"Not much," says Michael.

"He's scary," says the red-haired woman with bags under her eyes, who's called Jessica.

"He's determined," says Nancy.

"Ah," Katherine turns to face her. "What makes you say that?"

"It's the way he's walking, the straight line, the set of his jaw, that he's not rushing. He also seems confident. Like, if he wasn't confident that Anna would just stay there in that spot until he got there, he would rush a little?"

"Bingo." Katherine turns back to the group. "Determined and confident are two of this character's most marked character traits. We learn this in the first moment we meet him, and it's without those words being written about him. Good writing doesn't tell us, it shows us."

Oh, good grief, I've started to cry. I'm scrambling for my sunglasses in my bag and shoving them on my face. Tears. In all the many versions of this moment that I have imagined, I didn't imagine tears. I'm not upset, though. There's no sorrow here. Just a great upwelling of joy-filled relief.

Our exercise today is to profile someone, to write a scene in which we first meet him or her, and in a way that shows readers what the character is like, rather than telling them. I'm tempted to write about one of the people at the retreat center, but it seems like a bit of a cheat. Instead, I create someone new—a frustrated, on-the-verge-of-a-meltdown, tiny blonde woman who is slamming her laptop shut and scrabbling for her keys in her knockoff purse. As the story progresses, we'll see that she grows stronger and her movements are no longer haphazard, but sure and directional. She'll get a real designer purse.

It's trite, borderline cliché, and I don't care. This is the kind of narrative a lot of us are hungering for, the kind of storyline that we can see ourselves in, and be inspired by.

As our seminar wraps up and Katherine delivers her final pronouncements, we're freed for the afternoon. The beach beckons. Nancy and I agree to meet back at the center after lunch, and forty minutes later we're there with our beach bags stuffed with our notebooks, towels, and snacks. We follow the path that leads away from the building and along the bluff. Up ahead is a narrow staircase cut into the gentlest slope of the crag that brackets the flat land leading to the ocean. The beach is a forty-five-minute walk from the center, mainly along the staircase. As we walk down it, careful to watch our step as we navigate the uneven depth and width, the ocean and sky open up before us, an expanse of blues anchored by golden sand.

The earth beneath and beside us radiates heat. We can smell the rosemary and warm soil. And still, it reminds me of the places I come from, the dry, clean air of the Kootenays, and the way the trees would be warm to the touch. Arriving on the flats, we fall into silence, making our way past the row of cottages and toward the boardwalk leading out to the green-cushioned lounge chairs and white umbrellas arranged in two lines facing the ocean. We are the first ones to arrive.

Our server is the owner of the restaurant behind us, and she's quick to take our order for drinks. They arrive stacked with fruit and topped with paper umbrellas.

Nancy sighs. "I don't know how I'll get my writing done here."

But thirty minutes later, we're both immersed in our notebooks, lulled into a stream of words-to-page by the rhythm of the waves lapping at the shore. So we don't notice Michael walking toward us until we're each jolted out of the worlds we're creating by a spray of water shaken from his hair. He is sopping wet, and dripping like a dog.

"You're not wet. You each have empty glasses with nibbled-on fruit, and"—he pauses to take in the notebooks open on our laps—"it looks like you've both written at least five hundred words. In other words, you've been missing that." He points out to the water, and then sinks down at the foot my chair. Water seeps from his board shorts.

He's right. It's time.

Chapter 19

We're in the sea. The Aegean Sea. The saltwater buoys us and we're as agile as the silver-scaled fish darting away from us as we walked in, slipstreams of bubbles rising around our bare feet. Immersed in the nothingness and everythingness of sea and sky, a deep calm begins at my chest and settles out into my torso, arms, and legs. I'm breathing it in, letting it go, riding the waves of internal, eternal connection that engulf everything else. It's just me. This moment. This eternity.

The next morning, at the round table beneath the olive tree, the tears are back. But I'm prepared. I put my sunglasses on before I sat down. It's not the same engulfing upwelling as the first day, and in a few minutes it's gone. It's as though a dam has broken, though. And it's not that I can't stop crying. It's that I can't stop writing. Story idea after story idea streams from the playwright in my mind faster than my fingers can type. I've started taking basic notes, drafting outlines, adding highlights, and defining details. The characters are crowding out real people in my mind, and occasionally bumping into each other. Sometimes I forget which story a certain character lives in, and he or she ends up in the wrong story. Other times, they seem to make the leap themselves, showing up at the perfect time and place to shift the storyline and add a brand new depth.

Despite its stunning beauty, the beach is relegated to a very firm second place. The writers are a quieter crew than the rest of our retreat tribe—the second day, even Michael sits silently on his lounge chair, looking up at the ocean only occasionally to chew on the end of his pen, lost in thought. Margaret's voice booms across the beach as she strides toward us, but the moment she sits down her notebook is out and her pen is on the page. Jessica and the messy-haired man with the pocket protector, Grant, sit together but apart from the rest of us, sometimes quietly asking each other to listen to a particular passage they've just written.

Nancy and I sit side by side, lost in our worlds. Cherise, my protagonist, is stuck in an elevator. She can't go up, can't go down, and can't get the doors to open. It's all very stomach-churning, and I'm starting to worry she won't ever get out.

"Do you find it hard to remember that your characters are fictional?" Nancy is looking at me, one hand poised over the page mid-sentence.

"I was just having that experience with Cherise. It's like I've started seeing her as this woman I'm friends with—only I know her better than she knows herself."

"I'm so disappointed in Lucy. I've just learned that she was in an abusive relationship when she was a teen. I wanted to write a popcorn kind of a book."

"How will you write those scenes?"

Instead of responding, Nancy grows quiet and looks out to the sea, her eyes clouded and her face closing in on itself.

"Let's get a snack," she says.

The sand is hot beneath our feet, and we walk the boardwalk to the restaurant up above the lounge chairs. Inside, the owner is behind the bar, pencil poised over stacks of paper, her dreadlocks tied back with a golden elastic. She looks up as we walk in, past the tables for two at the open windows, past the karaoke stage to our left and the tables for four to our right, painted fish with gaping mouths and bugging-out eyes looming above them.

When we received our welcome info from Eirene, it included a long paragraph on what not to wear on the island, to fit with the custom here. No short shorts, no crop tops. Avoid excessive expensive jewellery. Whenever possible, cover your shoulders.

The owner's red lace bra peeks from beneath her white crop top, and the fashion lover in me calculates that her khaki shorts have about an inch of inseam, max. I'm a little in awe of this woman who so confidently flouts convention; I've seen her striding through the town square in the early afternoon, engaging almost everyone she meets in a conversation that almost always leaves them laughing. And she's dressed nearly the same way every time, acres of bronzed brown-black skin gleaming in the sun.

"Hi, ladies. I'm Lania." She puts her pencil down, ties on an apron.

Nancy speaks for us, ordering an ice cream sandwich for herself and a bowl of fresh-cut fruit for me. As she slices, Lania chats about the weather, the tides, the calmness of the sea today, and then asks us where we're from.

"Australia," says Nancy.

"Canada," I answer.

"You here for a few days?"

"We're at the retreat center." As I finish my sentence, she pauses her chopping and leans back to look us up and down, one eyebrow raised. Nancy and I look at each other, confused. "We're doing the writing program," I add.

"Oh." She laughs a little, shakes her head, and rolls her shoulders back before looking back up at us. "Here's your fruit."

Back out on our lounge chairs, we make a plan to explain why we're here starting with the writing program, instead of having it come in second. We're beginning to understand that it's not just the center's history of primal screams echoing down the hillside that the locals remember, it's the ongoing stream of groups who converge on their café sidewalks, at restaurant tables, and in the town square to hold each other and cry. The Life Learnings crew is constantly bonding over past experiences. They emerge from their morning sessions raw and tearful, arms around each other, shoulders drooping. We've started tensing up when one of them comes over to us; they've started approaching us in the midst of whatever we might be doing, to ask if they can give us a hug.

I open the shutters to sun. Tiny particles dance through the air, spinning and shining. The birdsong that sounds like a robin's floats across the breeze, and beyond the patio out front a dog is barking. Moments later, he is shushed by a terse order in Greek. They are sounds I'm growing used to, and as I settle onto my mat on the rooftop patio my meditation is easier. I sink into peace.

The days are falling into a steady rhythm. Morning yoga on the rooftop patio, breakfast at the center, our morning writing seminar with Katherine beneath the olive tree, and then the afternoon spent at the beach, scribbling in our notebooks and floating in the sea. And ducking the arms of the Life Learnings crew. That morning, though, during our seminar, Katherine announces a relocation for the next day—a walk up the steep streets to the very top of the hill, where a local artist lives and paints at an old Greek estate. Allan will take us. We'll have our seminar there.

Michael is leading our crew of writers up the hillside when he's overtaken by Margaret, speed walking with walking poles. "Good for you, Margaret," he calls out as she strides by. "We ought to make a chain and link to your belt loop." Margaret turns around long enough to raise an eyebrow at him and then continues her steadfast march up the hill. The streets are still narrow but the lots are bigger, with houses instead of apartments, and between them we can look down to the ever-present sea, still sparkling in the sun. These homes are white, too, but it's a cleaner, brighter white than that of the apartments down below. The front yards are often painstakingly landscaped, with rocks, vines, and fig trees.

But none of them is as elaborate as the estate we arrive at at the top of the hill. Here, there's a main house with a gallery, kitchen, living room, dining room, receiving room, four bedrooms, and studio space. There's an outdoor living space cut into the earth, the floor laid with intricate tiling depicting a scene from Greek mythology and a garden filled with flowers in reds, dusky blues, and startling yellows. On the terrace below is a crumbling amphitheatre, where the family used to stage elaborate productions of the works of contemporary Greek playwrights and centuries-old masters.

The artist, Karpos, lives here with his wife. We see her at the till in the gallery but he doesn't introduce us to her. Karpos leads us on a tour of his estate, pointing out statues in the garden, retelling stories of his family, and narrating his favorite scenes from the most notable plays they staged, years ago. He is old now, with a white beard flecked with gray, weathered brown skin, and swollen joints in his fingers. Karpos talks like a man starved for attention—becoming animated when the group is quiet and incensed when someone doesn't listen. He makes sure to speak with each woman in our group. Michael and Grant he ignores. The tour drags on.

Finally, we settle at tables in the receiving room to write and he has his wife bring us juice, Kourabiedes—a walnut sugar cookie—and homemade baklava. From here we see the streets we walked up winding all the way down the hillside, past the white homes, past the apartments, through the village and main square, and down into the port we haven't been back to since the day we arrived. Karpos sits in a chair, his eyes roving over each woman in our group, pausing at our breasts, hips, and the v-shaped dip in our sundresses. I shift my chair so my back is to him.

It seems like ages until the allotted time passes and we wrap up our exercise. Chairs scrape across the tiled floor and glasses clink together as we gather our dishes. "No, no," Allan interrupts. "He says to leave it. His wife will get it." I'm zipping the top of my tote bag when I feel Allan standing behind me. "Karpos would like to paint you," he says. I freeze. Across the emptied room, Karpos is watching, his head tipped to one side and the corners of his mouth lifted. His eyes aren't on my face, so he doesn't see me recoil. Allan senses me hesitating and adds, "It's a very uncommon opportunity." I shake my head no. I have seen the paintings of women in Karpos's gallery. They are all nude.

Katherine, Nancy, and Michael come to stand with me and then we turn together and begin our trek back down the hill. Up behind us, at a window in the receiving room, Karpos stands watching us go.

The next morning my hair is wavy again. I've had straight hair since I was born; it started out blonde but by the time I was in second grade it had changed to dark brown. Since then, every morning I've woken up with the same hair: dark brown, mostly straight. Since arriving in Greece, though, that has started to change.

Each morning, more waves have appeared, transforming my mane into a mass of corkscrews and undulating strands that form a fuzzy frame around my face. It keeps happening. And I keep searching for an explanation. Is it the shower water? The moisture in the air? The salt of the sea? I'm sure there's a logical explanation.

But each time I search for an answer, I can't help but remember something that at the time seemed silly and inconsequential. On the phone with my friend Fina before I left, I had said, "I want to come back with wavy hair." Always supportive, she had replied laughingly, "Maybe you will." I can't shake the thought that somehow just asking for it has made it come true.

Nancy loves this story. She's started commenting on my hair when she sees me, and that afternoon at the beach with our notebooks she grins at the mess it's in.

An hour later I look over to where Nancy is now scrawling fiercely in her notebook, jaw clenched and eyes glaring. Finishing her final paragraph, she throws her pen to the sand and slams her book closed.

"That must have been quite the scene."

Silently, she passes her book to me and I begin reading. Her protagonist, Lucy, is in a new relationship. She and her boyfriend have come home from a party. He is furious, accusing her of flirting with other men. The truth is, she was. And she knows he is sensitive, knows he is insecure, knows how much he loves her and how hurt he is. So when he hits her she doesn't feel betrayed; she feels guilty. And when he hits her again she doesn't raise her hands to defend herself; she begins apologizing, hoping it will assuage his pain.

The detail renders the images in stark detail.

"You imagined this?" I ask. Nancy shakes her head. "You're going to marry him?"

Nancy bites her lip.

The days have passed. Each of us now has our favorite spots in the town square, our chosen treat from the local bakery, our favorite restaurant to eat dinner at. The owners welcome us with smiles and lead us to our table. We settle into our chairs with a sigh, looking forward to the dish we've come back for.

On the last night, we gather after dinner on the Eirene patio. All of us, the entire tribe, are coming together for a variety show we've created. There are poetry readings, monologues, dancing, and singing. Last up is our writing group. We've banded together and written a ramshackle play. As my British friends say, it takes the piss out of everyone. Even Katherine.

I've been assigned the role of our indomitable teacher, and snuck into her room earlier in the day to steal (temporarily) her scarf and sunglasses. Just before we're set to go on, I pull them from my bag, hastily wind the fabric around my neck and stick the sunglasses on the top of my head. As we turn toward our audience, I hear her surprised laugh.

We parody everyone, even ourselves, having scripted Grant into the role of the hyper-observant, nearly mute writer who follows everyone around taking notes. Katherine has the most lines and the final monologue, venting about the state of the publishing industry these days, writers who expect instant fame, and the baffling selection of judges for the Man Booker Prize, who have not once selected her for their panel. When we take our bows, everyone is doubled over, some wiping tears of laughter from their eyes. Katherine is smiling when she thanks me as I return her sunglasses and scarf. "Although," she adds, "after that caricature of me, I'm not sure I should really be thanking you." We both laugh.

It's over, but nobody wants to leave. Karan, still in her linen and Birkenstocks, begins to lead us all in a madcap dance. We circle around and around, spinning wider and faster beneath a full-bellied moon until the stars above join in our spinning. All around us, the sounds of the night rise up. Dogs bark. The wind lifts and unfurls the leaves of the trees. Far below, the waves crash on the shore. The lounge chairs sit empty, their umbrellas tied tight. The restaurant up above them is dark. Out beyond where the water meets the sand, the moon shines down. And we dance.

It is in stark contrast to how I experience my next stop.

Chapter 20

There's an eerie silence all around me. As I lie in bed, it's unnaturally quiet. No footsteps echo down the hall, no voices murmur in the next room. No guest laughter floats up from the front patio. I might be the only one here.

My room at the hotel on Mykonos is on the top floor. From my window I can see the sea and the parking lot below. There are only two cars there, a red Audi and a battered Ford truck with a shovel, rake, and pile of dirt in the back. It's now early summer, and though I was warned that I'd be staying in a party town, there seems to be a complete lack of people who might party. In the dining room overlooking the pool, there's breakfast for ten or more. Breads, jams, hard-boiled eggs, plain yogurt with honey, muesli, porridge, and fresh fruit. But I'm the only one there besides the mustached man with lean arms and bony knees beneath his dress shirt and ironed slacks who strides in from the pool deck to ask how my sleep was. "Miss Lindsey Lewis," he calls me with a wink and a smile.

After the forged community and endless companionship of the retreat center, suddenly being solo again leaves me feeling a bit bereft. It's hard to know how to be alone, and I keep thinking of Joseph—his smell, the way I could bury my face in his neck, the taste of his skin beneath my tongue. I catch myself staring off into space, spoon held aloft. I wonder what they think of me, the man with the mustache and his sparse, friendly staff.

The sun feels familiar to me now and I walk out prepared for the dry heat that envelops me. Like many Greek towns, the town of Mykonos climbs up a hillside from the sea. The edge of town closest to my hotel and farthest from the sea is ringed with restaurants—each one with a patio far bigger than the interior. There is a post office, a drugstore, and endless shops. Around each corner another proprietor waits at the doorway, gesturing to the dishes, scarves, and t-shirts inside. The man with rows of gold and silver jewellery behind him calls out to me, "For you, anything in my shop." I shake my head, sure he is joking. "I am not joking," he tells me sternly.

The streets are alleyways here. No cars can pass through. I duck between white walls dusted with dirt and it's here, in the inner recesses of the town, that the people can be found. Cruise ships dock in the port of Mykonos and the flood of tourists fills the alleys and restaurants from morning to late afternoon. They stream through the passageways, Australian, American, British, and German accents dotting the soundscape. We step around each other, make way, and apologize when we run into one another—a sharp pain as foot treads on toes. The women in broad sunhats hold them on with one hand. I wander, turning each corner, entering shadows and then blinding light, winding my way through crowds that are like so many minnows darting and slipping through the sun's fingertips. The day passes and evening arrives, settling over the buildings like a blanket, and I am content after dinner to walk back to my room and slide beneath the blue bedspread.

Andy is looking me up and down, chin thrust forward, blue eyes defiant beneath sandy red hair. I don't know why he's angry. He's just come back from the bar, where I can see Iosif collecting five shot glasses filled with amber liquid.

"So, you and Iosif, hey?" He's leaning forward, both hands planted on the table, glaring.

I run the screens in my mind, flipping through the past forty-eight hours.

Yesterday morning. I wave to the owner of the hotel and walk the outer rim of the town to the marina where the tour boats leave for the island of Delos. On the boardwalk there is a man with a pelican on a string. He feeds it fish and lets men and women in loud shirts and cargo shorts take pictures with it for money. The fish are in a cooler piled high with ice. Each time the man opens the cooler, the smell of fish wafts out and the pelican hops forward, hobbled by the string around its ankle, feathers mottled and dull. The man has a signal he gives the pelican when he wants it to stand on his shoulder. When the pelican does, he gives it another fish. The men and women oo and aah, cameras flashing.

The shout of greeting from the captain of the boat that will take us to the island pulls us together around the ticket booth, suddenly frantic to pull out credit cards and cash in the face of his urging to hurry, hurry so we don't miss the sights on one of Greece's most important archeological and mythical spots. "You are only allowed to visit for three hours," he reminds us. Pulling a water bottle, guide book, novel, gum, and scraps of paper out of the way, a woman with an upturned, freckled nose, pale white skin, and blonde curly hair is scrabbling for her wallet in her purse. Hurry, hurry, don't miss out, the captain is calling out. The woman keeps scrabbling. Finally, she locates her wallet, holding it up triumphantly for the captain to see, makes her payment and scrambles on board, landing with an oomph on the bench across from me.

We watch the light dancing off the water as the boat rises and falls across the waves. The land mass we're headed toward begins to crystallize as an island, with two mounds of hill and a squat building with wide widows to one side. Delos draws closer. I'm interested in it because it was a holy sanctuary even before Olympian Greek mythology made it the birthplace of Apollo and Artemis. Before it became the meeting ground for the Delian League, before the Romans converted it into a free port, before it became a hub for slave trading, it was a place where people came to worship.

More than seeing the sacred lake, the market squares, the terrace of the lions, or the Doric Temple of

Isis, I want to *feel* this place. To see if I can understand why it became what it was, why so many Ionians made a pilgrimage here. I am making a kind of pilgrimage, too. And if I can feel what I imagine the Ionians felt when they came—real or conjured—I might gain a sense of kinship, a sense of having found something that's been missing for too long.

I join a tour of the island. There are only six of us in the group, but there's a tall, white-haired man with two cameras and a notepad striding beside the guide, scribbling and nodding, so it's easy for me to lag behind unnoticed. I'm watching each statue, each rooftop, each purposefully open space. I feel nothing.

And then, it happens. In the most unexpected place. A kitchen, protected from tourists by bars across the front and capped by a tiled roof. I'm standing looking in, the scent of dust and dry air settling in my nose, our guide's voice growing smaller, when a ray of sunlight stretches around the corner and I have to close my eyes against the bright white. In that moment, I grow small. And large at the same time. It's like being taken upward and then out, and out there is the realness, the beyondness, the freedom. I'm in it and of it, and this I know for sure.

I don't know how long I stand there. I stop caring. In that space the peace is all there is.

But I know when someone comes to stand nearby, so I open my eyes. It's the woman with the bulging purse. "You've missed your tour," she says, squinting at me in the sun. I shrug, still smiling, still joyful. "You don't mind, I guess." She shrugs, too.

The mid-calf skirt, short-sleeved blouse, and floppy hat are kind of stuffy, but she's around my age—from England. I step back from the kitchen and walk down the pathway, Sarah falling into step beside me, her purse slung across her torso, bumping against her hip. We've got forty-five minutes until the boat heads back to Mykonos, and Sarah is hot and thirsty. The air-conditioning in the museum cafeteria is cool on our skin. Goosebumps rise up on the backs of my arms. Sarah is traveling on her own, making her way around Greece. Since she's in Mykonos for two more days we make plans to meet tomorrow and go to the beach.

That night I sit on my bed with the shutters open to the sea. The setting sun has painted orange and pink swaths across the sky and left shades on the water below. Was there something special, something unique, about Delos? Could there be something a little bit *more* about certain places in the world? Why wouldn't everyone feel it, if there were? I envision myself trekking around the world, seeking out the holy spaces, the sacred places, the shrines to a particular culture's version of what I've been experiencing. And then it hits me. I can seek anywhere. I could go to a shrine or a McDonald's, a garden or a drugstore—and the place wouldn't matter. Because what I'd be seeking is in me.

When the sun shone around the corner outside the kitchen in Delos it didn't transport me to somewhere else. It helped me to arrive. When the feeling of lying in the grass with bees buzzing around me came over me in Notre Dame, it wasn't because of the stained glass windows or the height of the towers, it was because I was there. Truly there. Not at a particular place at a particular time but in a moment. And it was a moment of surrender. When I cried out tears of joy and relief during the yoga class it wasn't because of the yoga. It was because I had finally—achingly, haltingly, even resentfully—let go.

So. Yes. Yes, there is something special, something unique about Delos. But there is something special, a little bit *more* about every place in the world. And everyone *can* feel it. We feel it when we bring it with us. When we surrender to the infinite joy, we begin to see it in ourselves. And when we see it in ourselves, we see it around us.

Sarah and I spend the next day at the beach, lying on the lounge chairs, braving the hot sand on the way to the water, and either studiously avoiding or gawking at the boobs. Neither of us really have them, or have ever felt much pride in what we've got—plus, we're both from typically buttoned-up cultures—so this nonchalant penchant for going topless throws us for a loop. We're not really sure where to look.

"Oh my god," Sarah has her hand over her mouth, speaking beneath her palm, "those have got to be fake." What's interesting about the woman Sarah is looking at—auburn hair, blue bikini bottom, gold bangle, and flip-flops—is her nonchalance. She doesn't seem to notice the looks she's getting. She ignores the calls from men whose pale skin and eager faces clearly mark them as tourists. She walks with her face to the water, swinging her arms.

Since I arrived on Mykonos, I've had plenty of experiences that have intimidated me. While I was waiting for the bus here one day, a man noticed that I'd walked around to the side of the building and out of his stare; so he picked up his chair and moved it so he could still watch me. Another guy, this one younger and smelling of sweat, wrapped his hand around my wrist and pulled me close so he could press his crotch against me and ask me where I'm from. And the owner of the jewellery shop offered me anything in his store, for free.

At one time I would have read something like that, written by another woman, and thought, *She's not happy about it?* And then you're on your own walking through a strange town and it seems there are eyes on you wherever you go, and sometimes hands, and there's nowhere, no corner, no public space, you can tuck yourself into and feel safe. There's a famous photo, Ruth Orkin's *American Girl in Italy*, where a woman clutching her shawl and averting her eyes seems to race down a street lined with no less than fourteen men, all ogling or catcalling. She looks terrified.

I know that the woman in that photo, Ninalee Craig, spoke out about the misinterpretation of that moment of brave independence—in 1951, twenty-three-year-old Craig left her job in New York to travel through France, Spain, and Italy—but the fact is that when I see the snapshot of that moment it may very well be a snapshot of a bold, independent woman in Italy, but she still looks terrified. She looks how I feel in Greece, with too many eyes and too many hands and nowhere to go.

These Greek women don't seem terrified. I've see women laugh in the face of men pressing into their space. I've seen women turn up their nose and scoff when a man makes a comment I don't understand but the intent of which is obvious. I've seen women get hollered at and just roll their eyes. I am in awe of these women.

Which is why, when Sarah and I meet for dinner on a wide open patio lined with white lights, and a few tables over a tall guy with sandy red hair is elbowing his freckle-faced friend and nodding in our direction, I don't shrink away. I ask myself what a real Greek woman would do, and I sit up taller, take a swig of my drink, and shrug off the nervousness. Maybe I can grow bold through faking it.

The sandy-haired guy is Andy. His friend is Max. They're both from Washington State, so we have the Pacific Northwest in common. They bring their beers, and we sit at the table until long after the final bite of food, talking about places we've been, our funniest moments, and what we do at home.

"Yoga, hey?" Andy licks his lips. Looks at my feet, my ankles, my legs, my butt. Max grins at his friend. Andy adds, "I've never done yoga. I'd try it. I'm not very flexible."

"Yeah," I say. The server brings our bill, and Andy and Max pay it. Sarah brightens. The thought creeps in: *They think they're buying more than drinks.* I toss my hair. Smile it away. Nod at the woman I think I'm becoming.

We cross the street to the bar. It's only nine o'clock and it's empty. There's a table at the wall opposite the bar and we choose it because of its high stools. The truth is,

I'm spent. I look longingly at the booth in the corner, all plush and velvety comfort. Being a Greek woman is hard. I prop my head on my hands and let my eyelids droop.

"Bored?" My eyes pop open and dark eyes look back from a head cocked to one side, tanned cheeks and pronounced nose, with a lopsided grin framed by full lips. Above, tousled brown hair hangs in a messy shag that fits the sandals, Bermuda shorts and button-down shirt sleeves rolled up at the elbows. He is clearly Greek—no tourist would be dressed in a long-sleeve shirt in this heat.

"I'm Iosif." He holds out his hand and when I clasp it he kisses my wrist. "You ladies, and gentlemen, need some drinks."

"I agree." Sarah is nodding. Andy and Max are scowling. They soften a little when Iosif claps his hands on their shoulders and invites them to the bar, on the house. Max hops from his stool and leads the way to where the bartender stands, smirking a little and shaking his head.

"Do you think he works here?" Sarah is leaning forward, glancing over and back.

It's hard to tell at first, but after we watch Iosif and the bartender share a joke that ends with Iosif playfully punching the bartender in the shoulder, we decide he doesn't. He's a local who is good enough friends with the staff that he gets free drinks for whoever he likes.

Iosif has clearly done this before. He's not nervous at all—just friendly and confident—and the dexterity with which he has shifted Andy and Max from defensive and guarded to thankful and a little in awe is both impressive and alarming. When he pulls up a stool beside me and lets his knee lean into mine I sit up straighter and pull away. He just grins and hands me a cocktail glass tinged with pink. "It's special to the island. I think you'll like it." Wink.

It's the wink that gets Andy defensive again. He begins asking Iosif questions—one after the other.

"Do you live here?"

"Yes."

"Work in the area?"

"Oh, yeah, I'm around."

"I bet you meet a lot of tourists—women, especially."

"Yup."

"This a favorite bar of yours?"

"I come here from time to time. The music is great." Iosif turns to me. "I think it's time to dance."

Sarah is already out of her seat, pulling Max behind her. There are two voices in my head as I let Iosif take my hand and lead me to the dance floor—one saying "Be careful," the other "Have fun." We're the only ones on the dance floor, though a few other tables are now filled with people. Andy glares from his stool.

Iosif is a better dancer than I. He seems to be everywhere and yet completely contained, all at the same time. He is thrusting his arms out, spinning in place and taking my hand to turn me under the lights. I'm laughing. It's funny. But when he slides behind me and pulls my hips into him I pull away. When the song is over, I make a beeline back to my stool, Iosif close behind, calling out to Andy that it's time for another drink. Max and Sarah come back and pull their stools a little closer together.

Andy returns with a beer. He is looking me up and down, chin thrust forward, blue eyes defiant beneath sandy red hair. I don't get why he's angry. I glance back at the bar, where I can see Iosif collecting five shot glasses filled with amber liquid.

"So, you and Iosif, hey?" He's leaning forward, both hands planted on the table, glaring.

Iosif is inching back from the bar, shot glasses in both hands, spilling over his fingers.

I shake my head.

"He told me he's going to sleep with you tonight."

"Ouzo." Iosif is back, handing out shot glasses, settling onto his stool, lifting his glass, looking around and grinning. "Cheers."

I push the glass away, press his hand off my thigh, and shake my head.

"Come on." His arm is around my shoulders. He is pulling me closer. "It's Ouzo. You're in Greece. Have a shot with me."

He is inhaling, smelling my hair, the sweat on my skin, the baby powder of my deodorant.

Fuck it. I'm in Greece.

I take the shot. He sits back in his chair, corners of his mouth turned up, watching me. There's a taste in my mouth that isn't alcohol, it's something acidic, metallic. Inside my head there's a ringing, and a little toy train circling around and around and around.

"It's time to go see the sea." Sarah pushes back from the table, blinking as she sways, and pulls Max behind her.

"Yes," says Iosif.

He has taken my arm. His hand is papery soft on the palm and wrinkled and rough on the fingertips. As we walk, I pull away and he pulls me back in. I lift his arm off of my shoulders. He puts it back around. Is it OK to leave it there? Maybe it is just easier to leave it there.

The shutters are closed. The street is deserted. It is quaint and quiet, but with store signs the color of bubble gum and nothing else on, it is filled with dark corners. There are no other footsteps. Where is Andy?

"Sarah." She is not listening. She is giggling. "Sarah." She frowns, looks away from Max's face. "Where is Andy?"

"Who cares," she laughs. Max laughs. Iosif laughs and I can hear it echo in my ear because his mouth is close to my cheek. I can smell his breath—a mix of Ouzo, the saccharine sweetness of the pink cocktail, and something else. Spiced meat.

"Andy," I am calling out, calling from the middle of the street. "Andy!"

"Shhh. Shhh." Iosif presses his finger to my lips. Shakes his head.

We have stopped walking. We should not have stopped walking. The man with the mustache who sits at the front desk is waiting for me to come in. He will smile and ask how my night was, call me Miss Lindsey. I can't see where we are going. Up ahead, it's dark. I can't make out if there is a street up ahead, or just buildings.

"Where is the sea?" Iosif puts his hands on my shoulders. He is standing so close I can see a fleck of dry skin on his lower lip. I am biting my lip. He is coming closer. The fleck of dry skin is coming closer. Too close. I spin back, sideways. Where is Sarah? He puts his arm around my shoulder, pulls me in to his side. "Where is Sarah?"

"Come and have another drink with me."

I feel small tucked into his arm. I remember this. I remember what it feels like to feel small, to feel protected. I remember what it feels like to be held. I close my eyes. They pop open. There is a painful pressing on my right shoulder. What is that? I look. It is Iosif's hand, curled around and clasped tight, fingertips white from the pressure.

"Sarah. Sarah." I am calling, and the sound of her name is echoing through the streets. Overhead, a gull cries out, white against a darkened sky.

"Shhh. Shhh." He is pressing his finger against my lips again.

"I have to go back to my hotel."

"No. No. Come and have another drink with me. There's a great bar—it's just up the street. You'll love it." We are walking again and I am folding forward at the waist, my legs stumbling to keep up with the pressure on my torso. I duck, fold under his arm, spin, and start walking away.

"Sarah."

He is behind me, papery hands and rough fingertips clasping at my arm, wrapping around my shoulders again. Pulling me.

"Let me drive you."

"No." I am shaking my head. The toy train in my head has become a drum pounding in my heart.

"My car. It's just right over there. I'll drive you."

"Sarah." Where is she?

He is stopping me. There is a wall. I feel the cool slipperiness of the stucco on my back, his stomach pressing into me. He is inhaling at my neck, the spot beneath my ear. He presses me back, his hands on both of my shoulders cold against the wall and leans away, arms outstretched as he looks at me.

"Lindsey." It's Sarah. Sarah is calling me.

"Sarah."

"Lindsey."

Iosif looks away, frowns in the direction of her voice, and I push him and run. I am running and listening. Listening ahead, to where Sarah is calling from. Listening behind, for footsteps. There are none. The only sound I hear other than my own heartbeat is Sarah and me, calling out in the streets of Mykonos.

The next morning, I remember how the man with the mustache looked at me when I came in. "Did you have a good night?" he asked, smiling as though imagining that I had. As though I am like a Greek girl, bold and proud and unafraid. Instead, I feel ashamed, like a child who's done something wrong. I knew better than to have let it go that far, knew better than to take that last shot. I knew. And I didn't listen.

It doesn't sadden me that today I am flying to Athens. And then, after spending the night at the airport hotel, home. I am tired. Tired of the attention, the relentless watching, eyes and sometimes hands on me wherever I go. I long to walk into a café nearly unnoticed, to sit at a table in comfortable anonymity to wait for a bus without someone pressing their belly into my hip. Home. I long for home.

The chrysalis isn't stagnant. She is creating. If we were to project onto a screen the contents of her biological alchemy we would see tiny disc-shaped bags of cells turning into antennae, eyes, wings.

Imaginal cells. They were there all along. Sleeping. It takes a meltdown to wake them up. It takes the caterpillar growing out of her skin. Once she does, the evolution begins to happen in her body. Her cells are programmed to transform, to let go of what they were, to become what they were always meant to be.

It is painful to watch. Once formed, her wings are folded tight. Antennae curled in. Legs pressed against her body. She is struggling to unfold. There is nothing we can do. To rush it is to rush her to her death. To peel away the chrysalis shell is to expose her before she is ready, before her wings have grown strong through the continual pressing and pressing against her shell. It is the struggle that will make her strong enough to fly.

Chapter 21

Home. I have always loved this building. With its Tudor-style brick base, white and wood upper half, and charming name, The Rosewood, it tempted me each time I passed by—usually while escaping the place I was reluctantly still calling home. The gardens always seemed to be in bloom. The lawn was always freshly cut. And in the winter, red berries peaked out from the branches of a snow-covered hedge. *Imagine living there.* It was a fantasy.

The day it became my reality, four and a half months after coming back from Greece, I was out for another jog, pounding down the pavement in an attempt to clear the adrenaline that was coursing through my veins. The for-rent sign read "Studio Apartment." It was what I wanted: something small that felt like a nook I could tuck myself into. A cloister into which to escape from the too-noisy, too-much world I'd been living in.

When I pressed the button for the manager he jogged down the stairwell from his apartment and opened the door partway. I stood peeking through the stained-glass, inhaling the scent of freshly soaped carpet. I wanted to be inside, wanted to walk down the hallway past the fireplace with the French provincial mirror above it, wanted to ease through doorways capped with arches, and tiptoe up the stairs trailing a finger along the dark wooden banister. The entire place whispered, "Peace, quiet, calm." *Oh, I wanted to live there.*

Bob peppered me with questions: Why do you want to leave your other apartment? Do you smoke? When you have friends over, are they large gatherings? How loud do you play your music? What do you do for a living?

Oh, how I wanted to live there. Imagine an entire building filled with people who'd been subjected to that interrogation and told that since the building was old—built in the 1920s—and noise traveled easily, everyone was expected to be quiet. Imagine.

When he opened the door to the apartment for rent, I had seen in an instant where all of my things would go. I saw where I'd add a shelf, where I'd hang curtains, where I'd plant flowers in rows on the windowsill. I saw the birds hopping in the grass, the vines climbing the trellis, and the pathway to the birdbath. I saw the gardens I'd envisioned while reading books like *The Secret Garden* and *A Little Princess*. I saw myself, me, lying on the carpet reading a book. Calm. Content. Happy.

He told me the rent. My vision dissolved. It was too much.

I thanked him, and as we walked back to the front door he gave me his phone number. "Call me when you've had a chance to think about it."

Back at home I wrote figure after figure on a pad of paper, doing the math over and over again. But it just didn't work. It was too much. My freelance writing gigs paid the bills, but barely.

I called Bob to tell him how much I would love to take the apartment, but that I couldn't afford it. He paused. Thought for a bit. "What if I dropped the rent?" *What if he what?!* He named a price I could afford.

I gulped out my thanks, hung up the phone, and lay down on the floor. It was done. I was free of the music, the dirt, the Silver Fish that never went away.

A few days after I moved in, my new upstairs neighbor brought me tulips. Her name was Linda and she'd lived in the building for fifteen years. Standing in the doorway with her golden hair swept up in a bun and a richly woven scarf around her shoulders, she reminded me of an elegant storyteller—someone who had been places and seen things and returned with a well-honed sense of adventure. She was small. But strong. There was something fierce beneath the smoothness of her smile. I liked knowing she was right above me.

Chapter 22

He is taller than everyone in the room. With a wide smile. Big brown eyes. I've never met a man in orange robes before. He is radiant. I look at him and think, *He might know something about all of this.*

What had happened didn't worry me. Each experience had been so wonderful that it didn't make sense to make them into something to be afraid of or nervous about. There is a quiet moment when everyone else in the workshop has wandered away, talking quietly to each other in the relaxed murmur I've learned is a sign of people who've touched, however briefly, the part of them that is always at peace, and I set my shoulders and step forward. The swami clasps his hands together in front of his stomach and nods, eyes crinkling at the edges.

"I've had a couple of experiences . . ." I start. He nods again. "They were kind of like out-of-body experiences, or feelings of a lot of this uplifting love and energy."

His eyes light up.

Forging ahead. Let's begin with the most intimate one. There was a moment of great ecstasy. Of incomprehensible energy. A determined, delighted force that lifted me higher than I'd ever been. And it happened in bed. During sex.

It began as an expansion at the base of my spine and then charged upward, taking me with it. It was carrying me, lifting me inch by inch, touching every part of me as it streamed to my womb, to my pelvis, my stomach, my chest, my throat, my forehead and then out through the crown of my head. I felt my body heave and expand—a wave undulating from my toes to the top of my head. And then I was gone. I was up there, somewhere. All that had been around me was gone: my bedroom, the sheer curtains surrounding the bed, the duvet tangled in one corner, the man who sat at the end of the mattress, watching as I surrendered. It was lush, vibrant, heavy with nourishment. Filled with light. Radiant with color. Up there, I walked among tapestries richer than I had ever seen. It was a world away.

The descent was painful. I grasped at the scent, the beauty, the freedom.

And when I opened my eyes the walls were barren. The carpet was drab. The artwork was dull. And the sky was dark. To arrive back to this? Why show me all of that, only to bring me back here? "I want to go back there," curling up into a ball on the side of the bed. Instead, we drove to the beach. Sat on a log and watched the ocean tide ebb away. The moon was nearly full.

I tell the swami all of it—about the experiences in yoga, Paris and Delos, too. Everything falling away, a sweet truth washing over me.

The swami listens. And then he says: "To have experiences like this is a great gift. A blessing."

What the swami says next is this: "What you have experienced is a kundalini rising."

According to Eastern yogic traditions and ways of understanding and mapping the human body, there sits at the base of the spine a storehouse of something that can only be described as energy. This energy is powerful. Many books have been written about it: textbooks, stories of people who have experienced it, and instructional manuals on how to get it to rise. Each person who experiences it describes it differently—the impact differs depending on the person. But it's common for it to be described as masculine, as rising up from the base of the spine, as carrying the person with it.

"I think we should be friends," the swami nods. I nod. It will be months before I see him again, but when I do, what happens will shake the foundation of what I know about myself and my life.

Chapter 23

In the space in between that time and what comes next there are lots of stories. Stories of joy, of friendship, of losing my breath from laughing so hard, of nearly peeing my pants I'm so giddy. But the most pivotal one is about gasping in pain.

He sits across from me at my kitchen table. He hasn't taken off his jacket. I know what's coming; he is already dressed for it.

We'd had a fight two days before, in the bedroom of his new place. I'd dumped my porridge in the kitchen sink and followed him there when he left the table. He was getting dressed, brushing his teeth, combing his hair. It was the weekend, and after a couple of weeks without seeing him I'd hoped we'd linger, talking, sharing stories and laughs. I'd spent four months hoping for moments like that. Daydreaming that he would live up to my fantasy.

After our first date, I was more than head over heels. I was infatuated. He was an actor, a writer, and a bartender. We'd met at a friend's party. He'd emerged through the crowd to join me on the dance floor, and then spent the rest of the evening ducking into conversations or commenting as he passed by. Afterward, he sent me a message about how I was "a breath of fresh air." Could he take me for coffee? When I replied that I had just started seeing somebody, he told me to get in touch when the fantasy turned into reality.

When it did, I spent the healing equivalent of about three milliseconds being alone and then decided to look him up. I dragged my friend Brooke to see the play he was playing the lead in. He was magnetic, diving into his character's emotions, letting them play out on his face, through his body. He was smart. He was funny. When he walked off-stage, it was like the lights went out. I'd like to say the fact that he spent about half his time on–stage in a pair of clingy long underwear didn't factor into my instant crush but . . . I'd be lying. He was a star. I was struck.

"He's fantastic." Brooke was smitten, too. "He was the best in the show. And he's gorgeous. Honey, call him."

I *would* call him. I was an independent, confident young woman living on her own in a beautiful city. I would be just like my favorite TV show stars, dating an actor, going out on the town, probably meeting his fascinating friends at little-known emerging hotspots. It would start casually, and then quickly progress to true love. He would tell me that he'd never met anyone like me. And we'd get married.

The degree to which our reality matched my fantasy would be roughly equivalent to the distance between the sun and the moon. But I was convinced he was *it*. Which, considering we'd yet to spend more than one night together once every week and a half or so, was completely rational. But what chance did rational have against dark wavy hair, deep brown eyes lined with thick eyelashes, and the ability to quote from *Death of a Salesman*? Clearly I was seeing his deeper qualities.

I did try.

I asked questions. I mentioned potentially intimacy-inducing subject matter. I got nowhere. Each time I glimpsed beyond the entertainment and the presentation, he'd shutter. Cut me off with a joke or a half-smile, and change the subject.

He bought me trinkets—a term I'd never used before meeting him—and told me stories about his day. He liked to be amused, made happy, distracted. A sad or stressed Lindsey wasn't someone he was comfortable with. He didn't want to be the one I called when something had gone wrong. Or my sounding board when I felt stuck. I suppose he felt he had enough sadness of his own.

When I'd tell my girlfriends about my growing despair of things ever getting better, they'd agree with Fina's incisive observation: "He's very charming. But he seems like he's always playing a role."

I wanted to marry a man I didn't even know.

So that day in his bedroom, I sat down on the bed and looked up at him. "I guess the thing is that I want something serious, and you just want something casual," I said. He frowned. "I just . . . I want to see more of you," I went on, "and you're happy with less than once a week. I want us to do things together, to spend days together, to have breakfast together." He stayed silent, and I started to cry. And the more emotional I became, the more he shut down.

"I don't have time for this," he interrupted. "You can let yourself out." And he was gone.

I called him later that day and got his voice mail. It was two days before he replied to my message, and he arrived an hour late for the time we set to meet. When he came in the door, he didn't take his jacket off.

Now he talks about how we just don't seem to be finding ease with each other, that things aren't becoming comfortable. That will change, I say. With more time. "What do you think we can do?" I ask him. "Well, we can behave like mature adults, and end things without drama." I plead. I cry. I accuse him of running away. Eventually he stands, kisses me on my wet cheek, and closes the door behind him.

I lie on the floor. I punch pillows. I stand in front of the mirror and berate myself. My girlfriend Stella comes over. And in the midst of my post-breakup poor-me moan-fest, she reaches for something to comfort me and draws a life-altering straw. She says, "Don't worry. You'll meet someone else. You always do." The truth hits me like a wall collapsing. I am a serial-relationshipper. I am not a confident, independent woman. I never have been.

Fina confirms it. I call her up after Stella leaves and immediately launch my question: "Does it seem like from the moment you first met me I've been in a relationship or trying to be in a relationship?"

"Ummm. Oh, god, you know I hate being asked questions like this."

"I know. I'm sorry. But I need you to be honest with me. Please."

"Well," she pauses, "yes."

I groan.

"But you know I just think that sometimes we do things because we don't know any differently," she says. "You were in a serious relationship through all of your most formative years, with Joseph. You grew up that way." I love it when she uses terms like "formative years." It makes me feel like I am safe in the presence of a highly articulate—and free—therapist.

"How long have I been avoiding being alone and calling it being a normal young woman who dates? I can't keep doing this. It hurts too much." I can hear her nodding. "I need to get used to being on my own."

Before we hang up, I make a commitment. I will learn to unlearn my fear of loneliness. I will no longer use relationships as a salve. I will become OK with being just me.

My apartment is the perfect place to learn to be on my own. Tucked snug on the inside of a u-shaped building, I look out over a courtyard lush with vines and trees. Robins, chickadees, and Steller's jays pop in to dip their beaks and flutter their wings in a birdbath. They make me laugh. Fluffy racoons and their babies tumble up and down the fire escape to the roof. And every once in a while, a hawk lands here to rest. I'm mesmerized by the scenes outside my windows. There's a feeling here that can best be described in one word: safe.

And it's mostly on account of Bob. Bob is the building manager. But to me, he's a firewall. No unknown person enters the building without being spotted and subjected to a friendly interrogation. No unassigned items get left in the hallways without the suspected owner receiving a gentle inquiry about whether they're responsible. And nothing that needs doing goes undone. The building is immaculate.

Here, I sleep more soundly than I have in years.

It is the perfect place to take on new challenges and deconstruct an old way of being. If I am going to step off the cliff of what I am used to and out into the unknown, I want a cocoon around me as I do it.

And I do it. It is terrible. I feel awful. Every bit of loneliness becomes bigger when I give it space. Every unexpressed anger and sadness grows when I pay attention to it. And every insecure and self-doubting whisper becomes a shout.

It's Saturday night and you're home alone.

If you don't find someone soon, you never will.

You don't have plans tonight?

I finally, completely, and properly let myself feel the anger at Joseph. I'd been loving, had wanted to make it all easier for us and our friends. I'd wanted to be gracious and kind. Because a part of me understood that I had participated in creating what happened—his falling in love with another woman. But another part of me was aching. And I'd shoved that down each time it spoke up. Not anymore. Now, I let everything erupt. I pound pillows, punch the floor, lie down and yell into a sweater.

Then, I start to meet each moment of self-doubt this way. I don't shrink away. I don't avoid it. I don't call a friend or watch a movie or go to a yoga class. I watch the self-doubt come. And when it does I don't even wrestle with it. I look it square in the eye and invite it to do its worst. *Gimme all you got.*

And I realize that every fear, every sadness, and every moment of self-doubt will first appear enormous and unmanageable. But as I stand and watch them come, they get smaller. They shrink. And if I can stand and watch them, they will eventually disappear into nothingness. It is as though they don't have anything to latch onto anymore. And so they can't get hold of me.

Linda is proud. The day she'd come by with baking and I'd opened the door to my apartment and announced I had found the man I wanted to marry, she became very still. "How long have you known him?" The more I talked, the more her eyebrows came together and her lips set into a straight line. She touched me on the arm. "Lindsey, can I make a suggestion?" I nodded, head bobbing, eyes shining. "Don't marry him until you've known each other for at least a year."

When the actor and I broke up and I walked slow and stooped beside Linda beneath tree branches laden with green, she gently inquired about whether or not some time on my own might serve me. I was gobsmacked. It had never occurred to me that maybe the problem was not men, but me. It wasn't that I couldn't find the right guy, it was that I was approaching it from the wrong place. Like an empty room waiting for someone to turn on the light.

A few months into my practice of being alone, I am running errands. I have picked up groceries, been to the library, and dropped some clothes off at a thrift store. It's raining. And I realize I am happy. It isn't that I feel a thrilling high, or the uplift of joy. It is the absence of anything other than contentment. In that moment I am simply picking up groceries, going to the library, and dropping off some clothes. The fact that I am doing it on my own doesn't mean a thing. None of it means a thing. It is just me, being me.

Chapter 24

My friend the swami is here. I follow the scent of chai—cinnamon, cloves, black tea, pepper, milk, and sugar—down the hallway to the door of my apartment. "Chai," he says, in lieu of a greeting. Orange T-shirt topping orange pants, he is sitting at my kitchen table pouring it into two matching cups splashed with a red floral print. The tea towel he used to dry himself after a shower hangs over the back of the nearest kitchen chair. I transfer it to the bathroom towel rack, dampness on my fingers.

There is no chai like it. Nor any Indian food like the dinner he cooked the night before: onions and spices, potatoes, dhal, pickles and sweet side dishes I can't identify. There was chai after dinner, too. "Don't worry," he'd said, watching me drain the pot, "I'll make some more tomorrow."

He is pausing in the midst of reading the stars and planets the night I was born. The moon was lined up with Pluto—only a few seconds apart, he tells me—the planet of the unconscious. The lord of the underworld.

"For Pluto, for you it is not so much irrational or illogical thinking. It is fear. The anxieties that you feel. And, it has the power to transform you. But it does not come easily. How you allow that transformation is in your hands."

Brown eyes searching from across the table, he presses his palms as though in prayer and asks, "What happened when you were a child? There was something. I can see it in you."

There is a part of me that doesn't want to tell him. That doesn't want to tell anyone.

I was seven years old. Waking up in a strange place. My childhood bedroom. The same duvet, the same pink paint on the walls, same white curtains. All unfamiliar. It would come on in an instant—this feeling of being in the wrong place, confused about where I was, holding out my hands and wondering whose they were. It would last for seconds. Or minute after eternal minute.

My mom got used to coming to me when I called. Ready to greet a child who wasn't really there. There were family photos on the wall: me, my sister, Dad and Mom. I didn't recognize them, was frightened because a part of me knew I should. There was our living room: Dad's big chair, the plum-colored couches, floral drapes. I knew I should know this place. Knew it was meant to feel familiar, comforting. But it wasn't. It was foreign.

My friend listens, nodding. "This kind of thing can happen. It is a gift of grace. You were disconnected from the ego. It can be frightening because when you are disconnected from the ego-self, if you are not connected to this person that you are, you don't know who you are. You don't know how to relate."

He tells me that this happens when the self beyond the ego, the self beyond the mind, rises up and—for a period of time—takes charge. For that period of time, what exists first and foremost is our connection to the infinite, universal self. And we are confused. If we are the infinite, how do we relate to this finite body, this finite identity? Again, he reiterates: this is a gift of grace.

Then he drops the declaration that will rock me. The result of all of these experiences: "People's consciousness is raised just by being around you. You are a guru."

I do what any thirty-year-old woman would do when told she is a guru. I start to cry.

Chapter 25

What is a guru? A guru is someone who wears white flowing robes, ties a loin cloth around his pelvis, winds a turban around his hair. A guru lives in India, up a steep slope with a winding path walked by people who come to ask for guidance. A guru lives alone. In a cave.

I cry harder.

And then I get mad. Mad at life, mad at the universe. Who was God to decide I was to be a guru? Who was God to rip away my identity, to assail me with these so-called gifts of grace that felt as though my entire world had disappeared?

"I didn't ask for this. I don't want this."

My swami friend watches me. He says little. It isn't me he is watching; it is my mind. He watches it rise up in resistance, rise up against rearranging itself to accommodate an entire new identity—one where I am secondary to my soul. He watches the emotions play out, one by one. One by one they rise, step forward, roar out. One by one they raise a fist and stake their claim, fighting for their hold on who I am. One by one they lose their grip, and fade away.

The tears come and as they pour out so does my resistance. Half an hour passes. I am spent. The emotions are too. The chai has grown cold and I am ready for bed. There is little to be done, really. Simply to sleep.

There's a Buddhist teaching that says we'll keep being presented with the opportunity to learn what we need to know until we finally surrender and let ourselves be taught. Most of the teachings arrive as experiences we resist: people or moments we'd rather run away from. I remind myself of this daily as my mind grapples with this new understanding of myself. And I set myself a challenge, a way to focus on something else. Of course, it becomes in its own way a pathway to what I am trying to avoid: accepting who I am.

In the months I spent learning to be alone, I had made myself stay instead of run away from loneliness. Had made myself become comfortable with that discomfort. Then, I asked for something else. I asked to become stronger and more confident, better able to stand up for myself and be comfortable in my own skin no matter what the circumstance. If the truth of who I am is beyond what I thought I was, becoming comfortable in my own skin will be a very different kind of challenge than I first thought.

My external world is shifting, too, as so often happens when our internal world is transforming. In the same month that building manager Bob leaves his position, Linda also moves out. And a musician moves in. Well, actually, he's a photographer. Who loves music and drumming. This is something I learn the first day he arrives, when our usually sacrosanct courtyard, and my apartment, is filled with lyrics and beats.

My first instinct is to do what I've always done—ask for help and hope that someone else will come to my rescue. And let me just say that I'm pretty sure this isn't an endearing trait. But Bob is leaving, is pretty well gone. I remember that when instead of his cheery hello, his answering machine picks up. I'm stymied. This is an old experience and my response is auto-programmed. But now there's no one to call.

The only person I can turn to for help is . . . me. I need to sit down. This realization isn't reassuring at all. I have very little experience with staying confident in the face of, well, most things. But especially when it comes to standing up for myself. Just because I realize this in the same instant I see my pattern of avoiding doing it doesn't mean it's an easy road to freedom. I don't know what to do.

I consider going up and knocking on my new neighbor's door. Terrifying. I think about finding a way to get his phone number and calling him. Also terrifying. I know! I have the perfect solution. I'll write him a "Welcome to the building" note and in it I'll include a small mention of how quiet a building it usually is, and what pains we all take to keep it that way. I write the note, which leans only about five percent toward "Welcome to the building" part. There, that should do it. I seal it up, and then sneak quietly down the hallway and ease it under his door before racing back to my apartment. I have officially turned into a caricature of the passive–aggressive neighbor.

Of course, the note is very well received. Moments later my new upstairs neighbor is knocking on my door and he is *furious*. I'm not sure what he sees when he looks at me, but whatever it is, it's vile. Here he is, happily settling into his new dream apartment and there lands a "shut up" message. On his first day. And the girl who wrote it didn't even have the nerve to talk to him in person! Well, he's going to fix that. He's standing in front of her right now, making her face him anyway. And she's . . . well, she looks pretty much terrified.

He's taller than me, with fluffy curly hair, a worn–in T-shirt, scuffed sneakers, and distressed jeans. "Listen," he says, "I'm not a bad guy. If something is bothering you, just come and talk to me." Yikes. I'm mute. I guess this is what people mean when they talk about someone calling their bluff. I feel like he just told me I had to lay my cards on the table, and I've got nothing in my hand. I stand there just sort of nodding. I think I have completed a couple of full sentences. My face is flaming red. He closes the conversation, and then heads back upstairs. I'd say that went very well. I didn't faint.

Over the next few weeks my new neighbor and I have variations of this same conversation. Each time I dread them, and each time I make myself do it. I pick up the phone or knock on his door. I don't want to be a pain in the ass, I don't want to be the person who can't handle noise, and I really don't want to ask him to turn down his music. There are about, oh, a trillion other things I'd rather be doing—fascinating, fulfilling things like counting the threads in my carpet, watching dust gather on my furniture, or reciting the alphabet backward twenty-seven times. But I've finally—finally!—realized that it's either deal with this kind of stuff today or spend the rest of my life being upset by it and avoiding it. I've got to—sorry about this one—face the music.

And since this is such an enormous challenge for me and feels of such a magnitude that I can't handle it on my own, I ask God for help. Yes, I do. I say, "Please help me see in this guy something that helps me see that we're alike." Part of me knows that one of the reasons I find it easier to loathe him than to like him is that I'm seeing him as nothing like me. That same part of me knows that if I can find a way to see how we're alike, I'll dislike him less and be able to be more at peace with who he is and how he shows up in my world—music and all. And since God is apparently so benevolent that no request is too small, even from high-strung women who mainly contact the divine in a panic, God delivers.

The very next day, as I'm arriving at the yoga studio, I spot someone familiar out of the corner of my eye. There's the fluffy curly hair, the lanky frame, the round-rimmed glasses. There is my neighbor. He is packing up his mat and putting away his props. He's just taken a class. He's smiley and content, moving in that quiet, floaty kind of way that people move in after they've wrung out the stresses of their day. I wish I could say I was thrilled. Instead, I'm aghast. Not only do we have something in common, we have one of my favorite things in common. Not only does he do yoga, he obviously loves it.

I look for more things I might have in common with my fluffy-haired teacher in disguise. I realize that often, the music he likes to listen to is music I like, too. I notice that he seems to appreciate the trees and flowers around our building as much as I do. I spot him pausing to spend time looking closely at them with a small smile on his face. And, like me, he starts his day with a smoothie. I can hear the blender. I make a list. I write each realization down. And slowly, layer by layer, I peel away the mask I've painted him with, and start to see him for who he is—somebody like me.

The next time his music plays loud, I pick up the phone and call him. He comes down. We talk. We even laugh. It is only mildly terrifying. And I do it anyway. It begins to seem that this challenge, this terrifying experience, has the potential to help me align with more grace, strength, and even—if we were to understand this word as meaning something expansive and all-encompassing that has more to do with the giver than the receiver—love. Not the romantic kind. The internal eternal kind.

Then, another teacher shows up. And what he sends as a sign to let me know he is coming isn't music. It's a rainbow.

Chapter 26

He has hair like a river. Having hair like that must be like constantly being reminded of the power of the earth, of our connection to the winds, the sky, the streams, and the ocean. He walks tall, like something in him is constantly reminding him that he is strong. And he seems older than his years; there is a quietness about him that people who have been through tough things sometimes have, people who can watch what's happening and know that everything is still OK, because they've seen this all before.

When I'd imagined my trip to Arizona for a weekend workshop it hadn't included this. I had envisioned rolling hills, desert plains, wide open sky, and blazing sun. Golf courses. White-haired men and women decked out in plaid shorts and short-brimmed caps. Coiffed, landscaped, air-conditioned. It was all of that. And then, in walked the man with hair like a river.

I have to talk to him. It isn't attraction. It is a feeling of being pulled. And it is stronger than my shyness.

"Hello," I say. He smiles politely. "I just felt that I had to come over and speak with you."

He nods, introduces himself, introduces his children. We make small talk: the weather, the room, the chicken wraps and kale salad, and then I sit back down. Something is missing. Something has been missed. It disturbs my mind—a pebble being tossed into a lake, over and over—as the presenters exalt and rally and circle the tables. That night I write in my journal: "I met someone special and important today. We missed each other."

The next morning, he is standing outside the door to our conference room. Black hair. Straight spine. Definitive profile. Again I feel the sensation in my belly and chest, a kind of rising up and moving forward. I will talk with him; there is something happening. He takes off his sunglasses when I approach, and we go stand on a balcony. "There's something I want to tell you," he says. "Do you have time to talk?" I glance back to where my group is gathering again, coming together for our last session. "Yes." We find a spot in the shade and sit on the earth.

"I think you're the person I've been waiting for," he tells me. "There are six people who I've talked with about this so far. My grandmother told me to find seven." The seventh person, he had been told, would come to him when he was distracted. At first, he wouldn't recognize that person as the one he'd been waiting for. But the realization would come before it was too late. And so when he got home last night, he'd understood he needed to come back today. To find me.

From his pocket he pulls out a small pink stone. "This stone is for you. It's been with me all my life and has been a part of many special ceremonies. We put it at the edge of the fire." He places it in the palm of my hand and begins to speak Navajo—a language I don't speak but in this moment understand completely. His hands rise and fall, his head bows and then turns up to the sky. He calls it prayer talk. It is more than just words. It is as though as he speaks, the earth listens and comes to join us, circling around until we are buffered from anyone and anything around us. I feel invisible. And held.

I speak, too, saying things I had no idea would arise, things I don't plan to say. I begin to tell him about the rainbow I saw the day before I flew to Arizona. I was crying. "And then I looked up and there it was. It made me feel like something magical was coming." On that day at that time he'd been sitting in ceremony in a circle in the woods. He looked up to see a rainbow in the sky. "I knew it meant you were coming," he said. The seventh one.

The stone has a rainbow of colors within it. It changes each time you look at it, and when it's lifted into the light with great intention and awareness, it almost hums. I hold the stone for the entire plane ride home.

There's one more thing. A moment that doesn't make any logical sense. An instant where time and space and the laws that bind them dissolve. Again.

Chapter 27

There are little puffs of smoke in my living room. They show up in the kitchen and my office space, too. Out of the corner of my eye I see them, white and fleeting, hovering briefly before they pass away to . . . where? Where do they go? And where are they coming from? Of course, I've thought that maybe my eyes are playing tricks on me, that maybe I'm inventing the smoke. But why would I do that? Life can be challenging enough without adding in things that nobody else will understand. I decide that I haven't imagined them, and that it's not my eyes playing tricks on me. I don't know what's going on, and that's OK.

A few days later I'm on the phone with the Navajo medicine man. I tell him about the puffs of smoke. He says that on that day he was doing a blessing ceremony in the Arizona mountains where he lit a pipe and infused the smoke that rose from it with a blessing for some of the people in his life. As he thought of each person, the smoke that rose while he was doing the blessing was intended just for them. "I included you in that blessing," he says. "I'm glad you received it."

It's the last time we talk. The next time I call him his voicemail box is full. And the next. And the next. It seems we aren't intended to stay connected.

What remains are the pink stone and the memory of more moments that transcended logic. That seemed like magic.

Chapter 28

Over a year has passed since I sat on the floor in my apartment and made my way through my fear of being alone. When my friend Sheila asks if I've ever thought about what I'd really like in a partner I admit that I haven't. Except for when Joseph and I first met, each time I've entered into a relationship it's been because it was there and I was lonely. I was like a pinball in a pinball machine, racing from one guy to the next so I could fill the void in my life. Intention and asking myself what would really be best for me never entered into it. And I definitely never entered into a relationship from a place where I truly felt whole, like nothing was missing.

Now I'm there. Happy. I have let go of making the guru declaration into a big deal. I am no longer certain it has to mean anything at all—the turban, the loin cloth, the cave in the mountains. Being alone. The more I think about it, the more I see that my interpretation of the term is just as arbitrary as someone else's interpretation of me. Entirely based on perception, versus absolute truth. Versus everything that is possible. In fact, it was Sheila who helped me arrive at this place.

It was Sheila who smiled and shook her head, baffled, when I declared I didn't want to live alone in a cave—damn the universe for putting me in this situation. "Is it the universe putting you in this situation—or you?" My spinning mind caught itself and I smiled, too. It *was* me putting myself into that picture. I was creating it every time I thought about it. No one had said it had to be that way and even if they did, who cared?

I'm curious. What would it be like to get clear about what I'd really like in a man and a relationship? What might happen if I did that, and then kept being happy no matter what? I keep reading that the key to receiving what you truly desire and what's most right for you is to first see it clearly, and then do the next thing that brings you joy. In other words, you create the vision and then let go of feeling like you have to strive and strain and force it to happen. From a place of great peace and contentment, you do the next thing that brings you joy, and—usually—somehow, some way, with the vision held lightly as you take each joy-filled step, you get there. I've seen this show up in other areas of my life. I've never tried it with love.

Sheila and I agree to meet again at the end of the month. We're going to spend the weeks in between getting clear and intentional about what we truly desire in a mate and a relationship.

I don't rush it. For the first time in my life I take it slow. I make a list. The list is long. It doesn't include anything about what he looks like. I write things like:

self-aware, dedicated to personal growth, loving, kind, grounded, with a job he likes. I question everything. And scratch things out. I look at me, too, asking myself how I'll be in that relationship. How I'm willing to show up.

Years ago, a man with the name of a god taught me something about love. I sat in his office, sad and with an ache in my chest, yearning for a boyfriend. The one. Shiva asked me to hold out my hands, palms up. Into them he placed his cell phone. "Pretend this is a puppy," he said. I laughed.

"Go on," he smiled. "What would you say to it? What would you do?"

I closed my eyes. Remembered the fluffy softness, the wiggling bum, the eager nose. The silly fumbling run. Oh, there is such warmth here. Oh, how my heart expands and fills and spreads to the smile on my face and the space in my chest.

Oh.

This is where love lives. This. This place that has no end, that has no emptiness, no ache, no vessel to be filled. This place is filled with love. It's already there. It isn't dependent on anyone other than me.

I remember Shiva and his lesson about love and think hard about why I am creating this list. I step into this exercise with a willingness to embrace whatever happens next—even if it's nothing. And I evoke the feeling of love that stems from me. And the knowing that it is there no matter what.

The afternoon that Sheila and I meet is hot and sunny, with the kind of sky that makes you wonder how anything can go on so endlessly. We sit down on the grass and open our notebooks. Sheila goes first. She's drawn images and written words in different colors and the end result is a page that creates the impression that her mate is lighthearted, easy-going, loving, and free-spirited. Which makes sense. Sheila is, too.

My page has words. Plain black ink. Some trail over to the other side of the page. Compared to Sheila's it looks dismal. I read it out anyway, thankful for Sheila's smile as I say for the first time what I'd really like in a man and a life we might share together. He is self-aware, committed to growing himself, good at having fun, with a job he enjoys, a good group of friends, close connections to family, and a solid foundation within himself.

Sheila nods when I finish. Smiles her great big smile. "He sounds wonderful," she says. "I know," I respond, "but Sheila, look at this guy. How could he possibly exist?" Sheila looks me in the eye, lifts her chin a little, and says, "I believe in him." I pause, look down at my page. Then I figure, why not? "I'll believe in him, too."

In the meantime, I keep doing what I do. Riding my bike, getting outside, sitting on the grass with a good book, hanging out with my girlfriends. I'm on my massage therapist's table one afternoon when she starts asking me about my work.

She wants me to start talking about it, wants me to get out from behind my computer and show my face to the world. Starting with her networking group. She has her hands on my most painful body parts; what can I do but say but yes? The next week, I'm her guest at the downtown chapter of a national networking organization and Lena is introducing me to everyone in the group. There are about fifteen people there, including a chiropractor named Matthew. He's a bit taller than me, broad-shouldered, brown-haired, and broad-chested.

But this isn't the moment in the movie where things get all slow-motion and softly lit. Here's what I thought when I saw him: *He's not my type.*

But after that meeting I couldn't stop thinking about how he'd held my wrist when he talked about what he did to help prevent carpal tunnel syndrome, and the way his eyes looked when he smiled. And a part of me started to ask, *If your type is a guy who things never work out with, might it be time to try dating someone who's not your type?*

At the end of the week, I was on Lena's massage table again.

"You know the Matthew guy? What's he like?"

She stopped. Dropped her hands to her hips. Came around to where she could look at me, her eyes wide and excited. "Oh my God, you two would be perfect together."

I go back to the networking group the next week. Matthew's there. He waits until I finish saying thank you and goodbye to the director of the group—we are talking about India—and matches my pace on the way out the door.

"I'd like to learn more about your business," he says. "Do you want to meet up sometime?"

Oh my god, he's asking me out on a date.

Except it's not a date. It's a date designed as something less risky, and rejection-free. It's a date in disguise. Oh, he's good.

"Sure, that sounds good."

He asks where I am headed, and then offers me a ride home.

Over the next few weeks we send some e-mails back and forth. He talks about how he played guitar at his friend's wedding—*he plays the guitar, too?!*—and I mention what a wreck I am about being the MC for Brooke's wedding. He is sweet and to-the-point and I am getting more excited about meeting up with him. But I hold off. I want my next relationship to be different.

So I know I need to approach it differently. That means not doing anything just because I am afraid I might lose him. The scared-I-might-lose-him me is worried that if I don't meet up with him sooner he'll lose interest and it will never happen. So I make myself wait until I remember that even if that happens, I'll be OK, that I am really truly content to be just me, being me. And then we meet.

I put on a pair of jeans, a sheer white tank top, some moccasins. I figure, *If he wants to turn this into a real date, I'll let him know I'm good with that.* He shows up in jeans and a button-down shirt. Here's what he thought when he saw me: *Oh shoot, this is a date.*

We walk along the False Creek seawall. The sun shines. People on bikes stream past. He drops his coffee cup in the middle of telling a joke. We laugh about that, too. Then he walks me home. For the first time, I don't think one bit about whether or not it will work out.

In the car the day he drove me home I'd had an ongoing debate with myself. Because part of me knew that I knew him, had always known him, and would always know him. He was intimately familiar to me and I'd been here before. And yet, it was only my second time seeing him, and my first time in his car. *But still*, argued the knowing, *there is nothing you need to do. It's already done, was written out long before.*

Sunshine breaks through the clouds, yellow streamers between tufts of gray, touching the treetops, slipping between the branches, illuminating the leaves. Hundreds of shades of green. One tree stands taller than the rest, arching solid branches ever outward, sometimes resting one tip on another tree's limb. An aged mother. One branch in particular has stretched longer than the others, gives the tree the look of a directional beacon, always pointing. Just in from the tip of this branch is a bud, of the brightest orange. It wiggles a little. There is no breeze.

The bud shifts, expands as though with breath, and then begins to ascend. Up and away from the branch, away from the tree. Inch by inch. It is not a bud, but a butterfly. So bright she seems a ray of sun herself. So soft she seems brand new. She pauses, hovers in the air, and casts her eyes around her. She sees everything—ultraviolet rays that drench the world in a kaleidoscope of color. Up ahead, the light draws her forward. She moves toward it. Inch by inch.

Epilogue

There's a scent in the air that only comes out in the spring—a dense, weighted chord of sweetness that spirals out from a climbing vine with sticky yellow blossoms. Eyes closed, I inhale and pause. All around me everything exists outside my sphere: this place on the sidewalk, this pocket of air, this kiss of a breeze. I am savoring. More than that. I am settling into this.

Moments ago, I opened our new front door, patted the scarlet blossoms of the geranium beside it, and walked out into the world. Moms push strollers with flannelette blankets shading the soft pink skin underneath. A couple with two long-haired dachshunds walk hip to hip, each matching the other in shorts and polo shirts. The homeless guy riding his shopping cart filled with cans and bottles tips his hat as he careens by.

It's the kind of summer afternoon that people who live in rainy cities feel transformed by.

Over the past five months, Matt and I have been transformed, too. Deep into a full-scale renovation of our new townhouse, we realized we were also renovating ourselves. It's more than stripping a home of everything except the tub. It's a stripping of the past. It's more than the sawing and painting and choosing of colors and couches. It's creating the future.

We've been married now for a year and a half. The moment during our wedding when our friend Sheila conducted our ceremony on the edge of the ocean is my favorite one from the day. Rays of sun broke through the clouds and touched our faces and I couldn't stop smiling and holding Matt's hand. It was supposed to rain but it didn't, and our picnic baskets, white linen blankets, and wooden table piled with barbecued salmon, Moroccan feta cheese, Mediterranean olives, chicken skewers, and pasta salad stayed dry. Later, we toasted each other and our guests from the staircase of a log home high up on a hill, with windows for walls and the vast ocean and stately mountains framed there.

"Friends of mine who are married and still are or were married and now aren't have all conveyed to me the same thing," I said. "That it takes a village to raise a marriage. So, thank you. Thank you for helping to raise this one."

We've visited Costa Rica and Paris since then, and had gone to New York the first spring we spent together. Now a trip from Los Angeles to San Francisco and Portland is in the works. And next week we set sail with Matt's parents for five days in the waters and islands of the Pacific North Coast.

I stand on the sidewalk with my eyes closed, breathing beneath the leaves of the Spruce tree outside the window of our new home. It looks just like the one I pictured when I envisioned what our dream space would look out at.

Inhale. Exhale. Pause.

I am savoring. More than that, I am settling into this.

There's a part of me that wants to hang on to what wasn't, that can't quite believe things have changed. That wants to remain in partnership with fear and worry. She's not quite ready to trust this. Not yet. And so each time I hear her speak up, I pause, soften, and look around me.

Inhale. Exhale. Let go.

When I open my eyes, I see something no part of me can quite believe. It's Iairos. Iairos with his white shirt, cream loafers, and tanned bald head. Iairos with his crinkly eyes and bouncy step. Iairos who now takes my hand, beams up at me, and, after confirming that I am who he remembers me to be, asks—all of the years gone in an instant—"Are you happy?"

In that moment, the part of me that was hanging on, that believed worry was a life raft, lets go. In that moment, that part of me sees—finally—that the life raft was actually shackles weighed down with mistruths, and that freedom and strength lie in leaping and testing the water. I see it. I see it and I know it in my bones.

And I get to say, "Yes. Yes, Iairos, I am happy."

Thank you:
Cara Rawstron and Ashley Little, for your pivotal feedback. Editor Merrie-Ellen Wilcox. My husband, my sister and my parents, I love you. Mindy Kaling, for inspiring me. Gloria Latham, for the beginning. Nick Bantock, for books that made me feel found and a conversation that helped me arrive. Katie Proctor, for the good luck kiss. Sonya, Tara, Chloe, for being fantasy-land friends in real life.

About the Author

Lindsey Lewis is a former magazine editor. Before completely renovating her entire life, she was the assistant editor of four different publications. She has worked as a communications consultant, copywriter, and freelance writer. Lindsey has appeared on Urban Rush and Breakfast Television. She considers chocolate a food group and lives in Vancouver, British Columbia, with her husband, Matt.

Photo by Frances Iacuzzi.

Printed in the United States
By Bookmasters